RESCUE IN THE ROCKIES

RITA FEUTL

RESCUE IN THE ROCKIES

RITA FEUTL

NeWest Press

Library and Archives Canada Cataloguing in Publication

Title: Rescue in the Rockies / Rita Feutl.
Names: Feutl, Rita, 1959- author.
Description: Previously published: Regina, Saskatchewan, Canada: Coteau Books, 2019.
Identifiers: Canadiana (print) 2021017921X | Canadiana (ebook) 20210179260 | ISBN 9781774390399 (softcover) | ISBN 9781774390405 (ebook)
Classification: LCC PS8611.E98 R47 2021 | DDC jC813/.6—dc23

Edited by Kathryn Cole
Book designed by Jamie Olson
Typeset by Susan Buck

NeWest Press acknowledges the support of the Canada Council for the Arts, the Alberta Foundation for the Arts, and the Edmonton Arts Council for support of our publishing program. We acknowledge the financial support of the Government of Canada through the Canada Book Fund for our publishing activities. The original edition of this book was published by Coteau Books, and was supported by the Saskatchewan Arts Board, The Canada Council for the Arts, the Government of Saskatchewan through Creative Saskatchewan, and the City of Regina.

NeWest Press
#201, 8540-109 Street
Edmonton, Alberta T6G 1E6
www.newestpress.com

No bison were harmed in the making of this book.

PRINTED AND BOUND IN CANADA
1 2 3 4 5 23 22 21

For Shelah Kent, whose kindness and courage
make her the best Granny.

CHAPTER ONE

When she heard the latch of the heavy wooden door snap shut behind her, Janey panicked. She spun around, desperate to grab at the handle, to climb back into the life she'd just fled.

But the door was gone.

Even worse – the entire building attached to that wooden door had vanished. Janey turned again and frantically searched her surroundings, fear pushing away the anger and embarrassment that had led her to this point. She squeezed her eyes shut and opened them again. It didn't help. The mammoth, century-old Banff Springs Hotel, with all its towers, gables and ballrooms, had simply evaporated. Poof.

Janey took a deep breath, trying to calm the queasiness building up inside her while she figured out what was going on. Had she hit her head? Was she dreaming? No. This unreal landscape felt real to her. She was outdoors, but it was definitely not the wintery world she'd been in only an hour before. Gone were the snowdrifts from this morning, the smell of exhaust from the tour buses idling in the cold, the flurry of tourists taking selfies. Instead, she stood in a wide-open world, autumn leaves swirling gently around her feet and slopes of fir trees piercing a balmy, balloon-blue sky.

Despite the warmth, Janey shivered and hugged her woollen jacket around her, grateful that she hadn't taken it off before she'd stormed out of the hotel suite, desperate to get away from the weird stuff between Granny and Charlie and that stupid, stuck-up Max. But she wished she hadn't rushed so recklessly through the hotel, down a bunch of staircases, out a heavy wooden door and into – this.

Because where was "this"? Was she still in Banff National Park? Or even the Rocky Mountains? How would she even know? She scanned the valley before her. Hold it. There! Facing her was the same Cascade Mountain that Granny had pointed out this morning as they drove in. The small peaks on the mountain's left side always reminded Granny of a fan of playing cards held in someone's hand. Janey almost smiled. Her grandmother loved her gin rummy.

Okay. This wasn't so bad. She was still in Banff, facing Cascade from somewhere on Sulphur Mountain, which overlooked…Janey's heart skipped a beat. The other thing that was gone? She scanned the valley to make sure, but the bustling town of Banff, festooned in wreaths and Christmas lights, had melted away. She'd heard that the air was thinner at higher altitudes. But could a whole town disappear into, well, thin air? Not a single building or the smallest stretch of pavement to be seen, only a serene landscape full of firs, pines and bare-limbed aspen.

Wait. Janey's skin prickled. She took a deep breath. Was it happening again?

A few years ago, Janey had found herself popping into the lives of people who had lived decades, even centuries, earlier. But she'd been younger then and dealing with some family issues that had changed her life. Things settled down after that and Janey had come around to thinking that all the time travelling had simply been weird, stress-fed dreams. Now that she was almost 15, she was pretty sure that being transported to another time and place couldn't happen.

But this – this vast wilderness of mountains and valleys that seemed to have swallowed up every atom of her modern life – this felt pretty real. A magpie flashed past, cawing and scolding and squawking at the world. The magpie sounded real. The scent of leaves, dry and dusty in an autumn sun, and the slope of the mountain under her own feet – these couldn't be more real.

So what was going on here? Janey shook her head, trying to piece together her day. She and Granny *had* driven to the Rocky Mountains this morning. They *had* checked in to the fanciest hotel Janey had ever seen because they'd been invited by Granny's new boyfriend, Charlie. And Charlie *had* brought along his annoying grandson, Max. If you looked up pain in the butt in the dictionary, you'd find a picture of Max, all blond and sour-faced. Just thinking about him made Janey's anger and embarrassment boil up again. She kicked at the crispy mound of leaves beside her, grimly imagining his superior expression somewhere underneath the pile.

That's when a huge black boulder in the meadow on Janey's right shifted. It not only shifted, but one end swayed and turned toward her. At the same time, a breeze sprang up and Janey breathed in something foul and rancid. She stared, trying to make sense of what she was seeing.

A bear. A big, black, stinky bear.

Oh crap! There was a rule. But what was it? Was she supposed to make herself big and tall? Roll up in a ball? She couldn't remember. The gears in her head weren't moving.

The bear took a step toward her. Janey's brain may have stopped working, but her feet developed minds of their own. They moved backwards, turned and sent her bolting down the slope, dodging massive rocks and naked trees. Her brain woke up. Distance. Janey needed distance. She lengthened her stride as much as she could, imagining herself on a soccer field, running down a kid on the other team so she could steal the ball away. Or racing toward a finish line, the feel of the winner's ribbon against her body only a whisper away. Anything to urge her forward and not think about what was happening behind her.

It wasn't working. The bear was gaining on her. Its snorts and grunts grew louder, and Janey caught another whiff of rancid fat, this time mingled with rotten eggs. If she had to die, why did it have to be here, now, with this disgusting stench?

Fear and momentum sent Janey flying downhill at a speed and direction she could no longer control. She couldn't stop; she couldn't turn; she could only keep running from the danger chasing her down. But she was about to pay for this lack of control.

A large hole had appeared just ahead of her, a hole as big and black and stinky as the bear chasing her. A hole with a small fir tree growing out of it.

The fir tree was a puzzle that Janey had no time to grasp. In fact, she couldn't grasp or grab at anything as she raced down the slope. She was too busy trying to weigh her choices: bear or hole? Hole or bear? But choice was an illusion. When Janey tried to brake, her feet found no resistance, just a porridge of sloppy, wet leaves. Arms flailing, she skidded toward the opening and the tiny fir tree poking from it. Hoping to slow her descent, she sat down, hard. It didn't help.

Her feet slid in, then her body, and she was plummeting through the hole, like Alice, into darkness and a rising panic.

Her hands reached out, desperate to hang onto something. A tiny flicker of relief swept through her when she realized that the shadowy branches whipping past her grew larger as she fell. Janey grabbed at one, then another and another, until she scraped to a rough, bruising stop on a sturdy, but swaying, branch. She gasped and tried to collect herself, but the smell of rotten eggs swirled around her. She felt sick to her stomach. Janey shook her head, trying to clear it and make sense of a sudden piercing noise. Nope, that high-pitched sound wasn't coming from inside her head. Someone was screaming. And it wasn't her.

Why had she let her grandmother talk her into coming to the Rocky Mountains just before Christmas?

⁓

The key scraped in the lock and the front door opened, letting the chill of a November midnight seep into the room. Janey planted herself in front of the entrance, pasted a frown on her face and tapped a non-existent watch on her wrist.

"Didn't you say you'd be home from your date by 11, young lady?" Janey asked, trying hard to look disapproving. It didn't work. Amanda Kane only grinned, gave her granddaughter a quick hug and deflected the question with one of her own.

"When's it going to be my turn to pace the floors and wait up for you?" With her heels on, Granny bent just a bit to peck Janey lightly on the cheek.

Janey snorted. "Not happening. Nobody in the least bit interesting. Or interested."

Granny collapsed gratefully on the couch, pulled off her high heels and rubbed her toes tenderly. "What about Michael?"

"Why do you wear those things if they hurt you so much?" Janey asked, sidestepping her grandmother's question.

Her feelings about Michael were...complicated. Luckily, her question worked.

"Your grandfather used to ask me the same thing," Granny said, then paused. Janey knew she was adding up the years since he'd died, not long after Janey was born. She also knew what her grandmother was going to say. But at least it kept Granny from thinking – and asking questions – about Michael, the twin brother of Janey's best friend, Nicky.

Granny sighed, then smiled. "I'll give you the same answer. They may pinch my toes, but they make the rest of me feel good." She looked directly at her granddaughter, her smile turning into a wicked grin. "And Charlie likes the way they make me look too. He's said –"

Janey clapped her hands over her ears. "TMI, Granny. Too much information. I don't want to know what he thinks about your high heels." She was happy her grandmother was dating, but she didn't want to think too much about Granny's new...*boy*friend? With his grey beard and slightly balding head, Charlie Warden could hardly be described as boyish.

Still, she was glad to see her grandmother so happy. It had taken more than a year for Granny to recover from her cancer. To help out, Janey and her parents had moved from Toronto to Granny's small house in Edmonton. While her parents lived in the apartment in the basement, Janey slept in the main-floor back bedroom close to Granny's. Most times they all ate together.

The setup worked because Janey's mum was away a lot. She designed and oversaw the building of emergency housing for an international aid organization. Whenever a country had a landslide or an earthquake or masses of refugees who suddenly needed shelter, her mum was on the next plane.

Right now, she was in Cambodia because of flooding.

Janey was proud of her mum, but wished her job didn't take her away so much. Just before she heard Granny walking up the front-porch stairs, Janey had been in the kitchen, crossing off another calendar square with a big red marker. Only 32 days until her mum was back. That's when Christmas would really start.

"...and he's asked us to go with him!" Granny said excitedly.

"Wait. What?" Janey pulled herself back to what her grandmother was saying.

"I said, Charlie's the first guy they call if they need a great Santa Claus this time of year. And the week before Christmas, he has this special gig at the Banff Springs Hotel. He's their official Santa."

Janey could see how Charlie's beard and his deep, rumbling voice would be good for the role.

"When he's there," Granny went on, "he has to show up at all the events – a brunch with Santa, Santa's story time, the staff Christmas party and so on. The hotel gives him a whole suite to stay in – two bedrooms, two bathrooms and a central area – and he's wondering if we want to come along."

Janey frowned. Something wasn't adding up. "Who – you and me? You, me, Mum and Dad? Hold on. With two bedrooms, where are you sleeping? No. This is going into that TMI zone again, Granny. What are you saying?"

"The invitation's for us. You and me. In one of the bedrooms. With its own bathroom."

"But right before Christmas? What about Dad? And Mum? She'll be back by then."

Granny paused. "I guess your dad didn't tell you?"

Janey shook her head. She and her dad had chatted at dinner before he'd gone out, but the main topic was her lost cell phone. And he was still out. "Tell me what?"

"Ahh. Come sit by me, kiddo," Granny said, patting the spot next to her.

Janey chose to ignore the small seed of suspicion taking root inside her. She settled into the couch and pulled a quilt over both their laps. The furnace was on a timer, and at this hour of the evening it was off, assuming the family was all tucked in their beds.

"You know how your dad's office is going to close for the holidays," Granny began.

"Yup. He says that the way the weekends work out, he'll have nine days off. He's already promised we can cut down our own tree this year." The last part of the sentence came dangerously close to a squeal. Janey couldn't help it. Christmas was her favourite time of year, hands down. The lights, the colours, the presents…

Granny nodded and started to say something, but Janey couldn't stop herself. "This'll be the best Christmas ever. Mum'll be here – remember last year how she was stuck in Indonesia until Boxing Day?" Janey avoided mentioning the Christmas before that, when Granny had been so sick.

"This year we'll have movies and decorations and carols and cookies and…everything. And all of us, here together."

Granny nodded. "Yup. We'll all be here. Your mum and dad managed to get tickets so they could fly back together and land here on December 23. So I thought we'd drive down to Banff and stay until the 24th. That's when the kids at the hotel all send Charlie, a.k.a. Santa, back to the North Pole. We could leave right after that and be home on Christmas Eve.

I'd even let you pick all the road snacks."

"Wait. Mum *and* Dad? But she was supposed to be home the week before that. I'm counting the days."

"Well, your dad looked at airline websites this morning, spur of the moment, and saw a flight to Cambodia going cheap. It comes back in time for Christmas. So he decided to take it." She took Janey's hand. "I think he misses your mum."

Janey felt stunned. "Well I miss her too," she said finally, pulling her hand away to cross her arms. "And what about me? Why can't I go to Cambodia?" Janey knew she was sounding childish, but this was all happening so fast.

"It was a single ticket, Janey. He couldn't find another one that cheap. Not for those dates. He almost didn't go. But then I told him about this thing at the Banff Springs. Charlie asked me a week ago, and I'd sort of dismissed it. But this could work out for all of us. Your dad can go and meet your mum for a little holiday before Christmas, and we can go stay at a fairy-tale castle in the Rockies. It would be a lovely, lovely place to spend a few days in December."

Great, thought Janey. She'd spend her holidays being third wheel to her grandmother AND her grandmother's boyfriend. And they'd all be living together in the same place. Ugh. Was he the type of guy who stayed in his pyjamas until he had to go out? Or breathed morning breath all over everyone because he didn't brush his teeth until after breakfast? She shuddered.

Besides, when was the last time she and her parents were on a family holiday? Not for forever. She wouldn't mind jetting off to some foreign country. Was Cambodia hot in December? Instead of shivering in the Rockies, she could be getting a head start on her tan. And she could finally ride an elephant... Were the Asian elephants the ones with the big ears or the small ears? Not that any elephant had small ears but compared to the African elephant –

"...and Charlie has asked his grandson Max to come along too. They, of course, would bunk together in the other bedroom."

Hold on. What? All images of elephants vanished. "What are you talking about, Granny?" Janey rose to her feet. "How old is Max? Is Charlie only asking me to come along so I can babysit his bratty grandson? No way. How old is he? Will I have to change diapers? Or play endless stupid wrestling games?" Janey babysat a little boy who always greeted her with a Mexican wrestling mask and a head butt into her knees.

"I think Max is about 16, so I don't think the diapers apply. And the wrestling, well that would depend on how you two get along," Granny said drily.

"Granny!" Janey tried to figure out what was worse, feeling obligated to look after a little kid or feeling awkward around an older guy. This trip was sounding like way more trouble than it was worth. She was about to veto the whole thing, when she caught the wistful look on her grandmother's face.

"Your grandfather and I never did stay in that hotel," Granny said. "When we were young we could only afford to camp in Banff. And by the time we could think about splashing out for a stay like that, he was gone."

Oh sure. Lay a guilt trip on me, Janey thought. "Couldn't we just go on our own?"

"It's still a splurge, kiddo, and besides, this'll be fun, going with the official Santa. Charlie says there's room service and a fabulous spa. And it'll be all decked out for Christmas. I bet it'll be gorgeous."

Janey knew that if she said no, her grandmother would never say another word about it. But she sensed that the get-away meant a lot to Granny. Was it Charlie or the Banff Springs Hotel that was the real draw? Or was it the Christmas festivities? She knew that Granny loved the holiday as much as she did. Christmas was the prize for getting through all the gloomy November days.

She sighed. Maybe the grandson wouldn't be so bad. And maybe a stay at a fancy hotel would be fun. Her best friend Nicky raved about a fancy tea she'd had there. Would a few days living in the lap of luxury kill her? She could make her grandmother happy, maybe get in a day of skiing, and then be home in time to finally celebrate Christmas as a family.

"Okay, Granny," she said. "Let's go to the Rockies and take in a little pre-Christmas revelry. But I will pick the road snacks – caramel corn and chocolate balls and maybe some of those wasabi peas."

"Are you sure?" Granny studied her granddaughter.

"Yup. My taste for spicy food has really improved."

"I'm not talking about the wasabi peas," Granny said.

"Let's go to Banff. We'll kick off the season in style and then meet Mum and Dad back here looking pampered and relaxed." She eyed her grandmother speculatively. "Did you start dating Charlie Warden because of these Santa gigs? Were you just looking for another reason to hand out candy canes, Mrs. Amanda Kane?"

"Horse feathers," said Granny, getting up. But she grinned as she went into the kitchen. "I'm just ready to have a little fun." She opened the fridge to hunt for something to drink, which is why Janey almost missed Granny's next words. "You don't...you don't think I'm being a bit of a fool, do you?"

In the light of the open fridge door, Janey admired the way her grandmother's post-chemo corkscrew curls had loosened into a halo of soft waves, once again dyed her signature, impossible blond. Her grandmother had been so brave. Janey waited until Granny pulled her head out of the fridge, so she could look her in the eye. "You mean to tell me that a woman who's stared down cancer and won is worried about some bald old guy with a beard and a belly and what he might think of her?" she teased. "He wouldn't have asked if he didn't want you along, let alone your gorgeous granddaughter." Janey swung her shoulder-length brown hair to one side and swished across the kitchen.

Granny laughed, and the familiar glint returned to her eyes. She poured herself a glass of buttermilk. "You know, since your dad feels he can fly off to somewhere exotic, it might be a good time to hit him up for a Banff clothing allowance. I know you like shopping at those second-hand stores, but even that costs money. Charlie asked us to pack something a little more formal, like a dress, which your dad may feel happy to pay for."

"Devious, Granny. You're just devious."

"I think it might be one of those win-win situations," she said, as another key fumbled in the lock, this time at the back door. Granny and Janey watched as her dad stepped inside.

"What?" He looked a bit sheepish.

"So I hear you're bringing Mum back for Christmas..." Janey paused, "...without me." A little guilt wouldn't hurt, she figured.

"Oh, good. You know." He hung up his coat, then came into the kitchen. "Yes, I'm meeting Mum. We haven't seen each other in almost four months, and she needs help hauling all her gear back. I did want you to come along but there was only one of these really cheap tickets left. And," he looked even more sheepish, "our 20th anniversary is coming up and we're looking at this as sort of a second honeymoon. I've booked us a romantic little hotel..."

Ughh. Why did the adults around her want to share information she didn't want to hear? Was it the weather?

"Win-win," Granny muttered.

Right, thought Janey. "OK. So, while you're jetting off to meet Mum in some exotic place, the rest of this family will be spending some time at the swanky Banff Springs Hotel. For which, in order to keep up family appearances, I shall require a few interesting additions to my winter wardrobe."

Her dad looked at Janey's outstretched hand. "Am I supposed to kiss this or just fill it with money?"

Granny rinsed her glass in the sink. "Give the princess a little credit," she said to Janey's dad. "And I do mean *credit*."

He eyed them both sceptically. "This princess is still way too young for credit cards. But maybe a small amount of cash – to be spent wisely – is in order."

Janey did feel like a princess when they pulled up to the hotel entrance and two bellmen whisked their suitcases inside. A valet waited patiently next to knee-high snowbanks as Janey gathered her backpack and the half-open bags of popcorn and other snacks from Granny's ancient yellow Cadillac.

This *is* a castle, she thought as she followed her grandmother through the polished, brass-trimmed doors. The lobby was grander and more festive than anything she could ever have imagined. Two huge Christmas trees, one at each end of the enormous entrance, twinkled with red ribbons, white snowflakes and masses of fairy lights. Evergreen garlands and gold ribbon stretched across archways and dripped from doorways, while dozens of poinsettias brightened every corner. A harpist teased "Deck the Halls" from her instrument, while three little boys argued about how to spell *reindeer* at Santa's mailbox. Two – two! – gingerbread houses stood against the walls, one a sweet-toothed version of Santa's cottage, and the other a replica of the hotel.

"Look at the work on this," Janey said, marvelling at the medallions and small, intricately designed animals.

"Thank goodness our rooms aren't in there," Granny said, nodding at the gingerbread hotel. "I'd gain 10 pounds just breathing it all in." She turned and walked toward the front desk, her heels on the slate floor announcing their arrival with a slow drum roll.

"We're staying with Charles Warden," she said.

"Ah," said the young woman, smiling at them both. Then she dropped her voice. "Welcome to the Banff Springs, Mrs. Claus."

"Oh, no, I'm not...I mean, we're not...."

Janey smirked. It was fun watching Granny get flustered.

"Our bellman will show you the way," the woman said, handing one card key to Granny and another to Janey, who set down a half-open bag of caramel corn to take it.

"Sam could carry that up for you," the woman said, nodding at the popcorn.

"I'm okay," said Janey, grabbing her things and turning to her grandmother. "Let's go, Mrs. Claus. Mustn't keep the bellman waiting."

Granny said nothing, but strode across the lobby to the elevator so fast that Janey almost trotted to keep up. Unfazed, the bellman gathered their luggage and floated along behind them.

When the elevator doors closed, Granny turned to Janey. "Do I look like a fat little old lady with a bun of white hair?"

The bellman kept his eyes glued to the floor numbers above the door, but Janey could tell he was trying not to smile. "No Granny. You look like someone about to meet your boyfriend." Granny glared at her. It dawned on Janey that her grandmother might be as nervous about this stay as she was. Would everyone behave? Would the boys – Max *and* Charlie – be fun to spend these next few days with?

The elevator finally reached their floor. At the end of the hall, Charlie Warden peeked from the door.

"Amanda!" he said, rushing out and sweeping Granny into a big hug. He ushered everyone inside, tipped the bellman and shut the door firmly behind them.

"I'm so happy you're finally here," he said, clasping Granny to him and planting a kiss on her lips.

"Charlie! Stop it," Granny said, giggling as she squeezed him back. Giggling?! This was a first, Janey thought. She'd heard her grandmother laugh, snort, even guffaw, but never giggle. Ever. And here she was, acting like a…a teenager, in a full-bodied clasp that was dragging on and on. Had Janey miscalculated the relationship between them? Were the next few days going to be way more awkward than she'd imagined? Caught between the door and the couple, Janey tried to look away, but it was like not staring at a car accident. Determined, she peered past them to take in the suite. She sensed, more than saw, the spaciousness and the sunlight pouring in through the windows. Charlie finally broke the clutch and turned to her.

"And Janey! I'm so glad I'll be spending some time getting to know you properly, instead of only nodding to you when I pick up Amanda. Though she's told me so much about you that I feel that we're old friends already." He gathered her and her bundles into another big hug. Thankfully it was much shorter than Granny's.

Janey studied him after he stepped back. He'd grown an even longer beard since she'd last seen him and she had to admit it was perfect for his role, flowing down his shirt like a soft, white bandana. He was solidly built, but not really that fat. He probably needed to pad his belly when he put on the red suit, she realized. No wonder Granny liked spending time with him.

"And this is Max, my grandson. He's spending the holidays with me," Charlie said. Janey and Granny nodded at the figure standing by the window, thumbing through a cell phone. Max finally tucked it into his back pocket, came over and shook Granny's hand stiffly, his expression unreadable.

"We'll let you young people introduce yourselves. I have so much to catch you up on, Amanda," Charlie said, whisking Granny into the living room, where they stood holding hands and almost whispering. Yuck, thought Janey. Was this how it was going to be, watching as two old people couldn't keep their hands off each other? Granny should have warned her. But wait. They were both frowning. Odd –

"Hello. I am Max."

Janey tore her eyes away from the scene in the living room to the guy in front of her, his right hand thrust out, waiting for Janey to shake it. Flustered, she put out her own, and dropped the bag of caramel corn. It scattered impressively around their feet. A wave of embarrassment washed over her as she stooped to collect the mess. This allowed the bag of wasabi peas and the foil-wrapped chocolate balls in her other hand to explode all over the hallway tiles.

She groaned. Could the floor please open and swallow her up? Could she back out of here right now?

"Everything okay over there?" Granny asked.

"No, no, it's all right," she mumbled, not looking up.

"Are you sure?"

"Yeah Granny. I just, just, did the traditional Kane blessing of the hotel room with road snacks," she called out, grabbing wildly at the runaway chocolates and wasabi peas that were rolling, like manic marbles, around Max's feet. Why did all of her favourite snacks have to be so round? At least the jawbreakers had stayed in the plastic zip bag in her coat pocket.

The adults returned to their own conversation.

"This is a Canadian custom?"

What? Reluctantly she looked up. Max was still standing there, looking down at her, obviously too cool to help someone as awkward and dorky as her. Sweat was gathering on the palms of her hands and the caramel corn and wasabi peas were sticking to them. She rose to her feet, trying to brush them off. This was hopeless.

"Well, is it? It's very messy."

"No," she snapped. "It's not a Canadian custom. I..." She took a deep breath. "Let's start again. I'm Janey."

"Yes," he said. He was taller than her, with eyes the colour of a bright winter sky. Were they laughing at her? No, they looked oddly flat and guarded. Was he regretting that his grandfather had asked them to come? Was he thinking she was a loser who made major messes and he'd be stuck with her? "And I am Max."

Janey's ear picked up the slightest of accents.

"German?" she asked, trying to move the conversation away from the disaster around their feet.

"Well, I speak it, but I am from Austria," he said. "It's like the people here. They speak English, but they're Canadian."

Well yeah, thought Janey, secretly trying to pick a piece of caramel corn from between her fingers. I know that. A wasabi pea worked its way loose from Janey's hands and clattered onto the floor. Mortified and unsure of what to do, she looked past Max to where Granny and Charlie had settled on the couch, still talking, foreheads almost touching. Granny was frowning and saying something. She was probably apologizing for bringing her klutzy granddaughter.

"I also know French and Latin," Max went on.

Her attention shot back to him. Was he boasting? Trying to put her in her place with all his languages? "I wasn't asking about your nationality," Janey said. "I was just trying to make conversation."

"So was I." They stared at each other. His back pocket buzzed and Max whipped out his phone. Now he was frowning too.

Fine, thought Janey, crouching down to deal with the fiasco on the floor. She'd clean it up and slink away to hide in a bedroom for the next four days while Granny and Charlie had their fling and ol' Max here did whatever he needed to do, far away from her. Her backpack was full of books. She would survive. Then she and Granny could go home and this would all be a bad dream.

But the bad dream was feeling too real, as chocolate balls and wasabi peas suddenly came skittering toward her. Perfect.

Now the snacks were alive, coming to attack her. More and more of them. She looked up from the floor – would she ever get past this entryway? – to see Max using a hotel menu to sweep everything toward her. He set a garbage can down beside her and together they gathered up the treats.

Let's try this a third time, Janey thought. "My mum's family was from Austria," she said finally, collecting the last bits into a bag. "Her dad came over to Canada a long time ago."

"So, you speak German too?"

"Well, just a few words. But I take French. And I can do Spanish once I get to high school." Janey felt a defensive note creep into her voice. Just because he could speak half a dozen languages didn't mean she –

"Ah yes. You are still in what is called junior high here?"

What did he mean by *still*? Was he putting her in her place because she was so much younger than him? "Yes. I'm in Grade 9. What grade are you in?"

"I'm in my 10th year of schooling at a Gymnasium in Vienna."

Janey gathered the last of the snacks and stood up. "You're studying to be a gymnast? Wow. That's cool." He was tall and wiry enough. She had no problems imagining him jackknifing through rings or over bars.

"A Gymnasium is like a high school here. I don't do gymnastics," Max said. Was that a smirk? Could she get nothing right with this guy? How was she supposed to know how schools over there worked? Something in her expression must have caught his eye. "But I love to ski," he went on quickly. "That's why I'm here. To see whether your Rocky Mountains are as good as our Alps."

"Well good luck with that," Janey said and brushed past. She'd had enough of Max. What did he mean, *her* Rocky Mountains being as good as *his* stupid Alps? She made her way to the empty couch opposite Granny and Charlie. They pulled apart almost guiltily, though Charlie still held one of Granny's hands. My nun's habit must be showing, Janey thought as she plopped down into soft cushions.

"Well," said Charlie, obviously searching for something they could all talk about. "Did I...did you charming ladies remember to bring your dancing shoes? The Christmas ball for the staff is on Wednesday night, and since the public isn't invited, I get to bring a date. You did pack something formal, right?"

Oh yeah, Janey thought. They'd each brought something fancy. She and Granny barely ever argued, but they'd nearly come to blows after Granny pulled out a long green dress from a rack at Janey's favourite second-hand store.

"But it looks great and it picks up the colour of your eyes," Granny had said, holding it up under Janey's chin.

"What on earth do I need a long dress for, Granny? And why would I spend a whack of money on something that's only for Christmas?"

"I pulled this off the sales rack. It's not a Christmas dress. It's an anytime dress and it's marked down so far that they're practically paying us to take it."

"But they're hard to walk in and Nicky says if you're tall, a long dress just makes you look taller. I don't want it." Only after Michael's growth spurt last summer did Janey realize she could stop slouching so she wouldn't tower over him, or any other guy, for that matter.

"Kiddo, your being tall means you get to see eye to eye

with any boy who thinks he can pull something over on you. Don't knock being tall."

"But I –"

"C'mon, Janey. Just try it on."

And that's why Janey had a floor-length dress crammed into the bottom of her bag.

"I know how much you like to dance, Amanda, so I've ordered some special songs." Charlie stood up, pulled Granny onto her feet and twirled her across the large living room. They were smiling again. Charlie must have accepted Granny's apology for the garbage Janey had spilled all over the floor.

"To start the dance each year Santa gets to pick the loveliest lady in the room for his partner. And I've got her right here," he said.

"Hang on a minute, Charlie," Granny said, even as he twirled her away from him. She was giggling again.

"For longer than a minute," Charlie said, pulling her back and holding her close.

This wasn't a single-car fender-bender kind of accident, Janey thought. This was one of those huge, 10-car pileups with sirens wailing and lights flashing. She forced herself to look away, and caught the severe, unsmiling expression on Max's face. He was checking his phone again. He was either just as embarrassed as she was by their grandparents, she decided, or he was bored out of his mind by a kid who couldn't speak five languages but could manage to make a massive mess within five seconds of meeting him.

Or the whole thing was a setup for a video of most embarrassing moments. She wondered if she should check for hidden cameras.

"I even ordered a Viennese waltz so Max could show off his moves," Charlie said, finally releasing her grandmother. "How's your waltzing, Janey? Max is pretty good. He gets it from his grandfather."

"Yes," said Max, looking up from his phone. "But we also learn at school. Before Gymnasium." He said the last word pointedly.

Oh no, thought Janey. Granny had NOT told her anything about doing a waltz. Especially with this stuck-up, disapproving Captain Buzzkill standing there, scowling at her. How was all this happening? She had to get out of here. She rose and skirted past Max, not seeing a small, twinkling Christmas tree until she brushed against it. It teetered, the red balls swaying precariously. They probably wanted to join the car snacks, Janey thought miserably, feeling clumsy and stupid and desperate for a quiet place to pull herself together. She took the first door she found.

"Sorry. No. That's my bedroom. Well, mine and my grandfather's."

Janey spun around, trying to leave, only to crash into Max. Stepping back, she lost her footing. Max grabbed her with both hands.

"Hey you two! Practising your dance moves already? Good for you. Glad to see you're getting along so well," Charlie said, coming up behind them. He nodded at something on the dresser. "Now's probably the right time, Max."

Janey shook her hands free. What did Charlie mean? Did he think that she and Max were...what? Making out? Moments after meeting? Just because her grandmother was acting like a teenager didn't mean that she... "We weren't...this isn't..." she tried to explain, her face flushing. She gave up.

"Where's the bedroom I'm staying in?" She wanted out of here.

"Hang on a second, Janey. I'll show you your bedroom in just a minute. But first, we thought – I mean, Max has something for you." Janey could feel something small and boxlike being thrust into her hands. That's when Granny came up behind him.

"Hey kiddo, no hanging around the boys' bedroom," she said. She was smiling, unlike Max, who stood to the side, looking on in complete disapproval.

This had to end.

Janey shoved past them all, hoping to find her bedroom. Instead, she pulled open the door into the hallway, the one she'd entered 30 klutzy and humiliating minutes earlier. No way was she turning back to face even more embarrassment. She rushed out along the hallway, found the door to the stairwell and flew down one set of stairs after another, wanting only to get away. At the bottom of one particularly long flight, Janey realized she was still holding the box Max had shoved at her. He'd probably been forced into it, she realized, his disapproving face flashing through her mind. She swore – at Max, at the last half hour, at the world – and stuffed the box into her coat pocket before pushing open a heavy wooden door into…nothing.

Make that nothing with a bear, a tiny tree, a plunge down a hole and someone's screams, now dying away.

"Hello?" Janey called into the darkness. "Is anyone here?" Her words sounded as if they'd rushed off to bang against a faraway wall before returning, familiar but fading, until silence took over. "Hello?" she called again, but quieter, almost a whisper. In response, a swish of water charged toward her.

CHAPTER TWO

Something hard poked into Janey's side. Startled, she grabbed the branch above her to pull herself away from whatever was prodding at her.

"Who are you?" The voice was low and urgent. "Where do you come from? How many are you?"

"I'm…I'm Janey. Janey Kane," she said, willing her eyes to take in her surroundings. It wasn't completely dark, she realized. Light trickled in from the hole overhead and she could make out someone standing below her. "There's only me. I'm the only one. Who are you? How many are you?"

Water sloshed as the figure shifted the pole used to poke at Janey from one hand to another. "Are you a woman?"

Janey considered her answer. She was definitely in some sort of a weird time or place, if the person below couldn't tell that her name was a girl's. If she'd time-travelled into the past, she knew that passing herself off as male would give her more freedom. After all, she was wearing a white T-shirt with jeans, a plain sweater and hiking boots. Her blue wool jacket looked a lot like one that had belonged to her grandfather when he was a boy. She could get away with saying she was a guy. But something in the question made Janey realize that the person below was a girl. A girl in a pool, with hardly any clothes on, brandishing a pole long enough to do some real damage.

"I'm a girl, like you," she said, trying to read the expression on her inquisitor's face through the steam that swirled around them. Janey's T-shirt was beginning to stick to the small of her back, and she realized that the temperature here was way warmer than what she'd left with the bear. She pulled off her jacket, careful not to let it drop into the pool below. "Who are you?"

"But you wear trousers." The stick poked at Janey's black jeans. "*Îyethka Nakoda* girls wear dresses or skirts. Even white girls wear dresses. How can you be a girl?"

The heat was stifling. Janey yanked off her sweater and felt a little better. "I'm a girl who likes to wear trousers...or pants," she said. "Who are you?" she asked again. "What's your name?"

The girl drew herself up. "My English name is Mary. I am of the *Îyethka Nakoda* – the people who speak a clear language. Your people call us the Stoney Nakoda." She eyed Janey. "I think you are not a boy. Or a girl. I think you are a magpie. All blue and black and white." Here she poked at Janey's white T-shirt again. But Janey sensed it wasn't quite as ferocious a poke. "A foolish magpie who flies into a place where a girl is alone."

It would be creepy to have something crash into her solo pool party, Janey thought. "Look, I'm sorry I scared you. But I'm not a magpie. I'm a girl who was chased by a bear and fell down a hole. I sure hope he doesn't come down here."

Mary studied her, then grinned. "The bear never chases the magpie. You cannot be a magpie then, even though you wear a magpie's colours. And bears do not climb down here. They do not like the smell."

Janey could see – or smell – the bears' point. It really did stink in here. This place must be the source of the rotten-egg stench she'd noticed while she was running down the hill. Oddly, the longer she sat here, the less it bothered her. What were literally becoming a pain in the butt were the needles poking up from the branch she was sitting on. When she shifted her weight, the whole tree moved. The fir tree, she realized, wasn't some outgrowth from the pool below, but a makeshift ladder to climb in and out of the opening. What she had seen during her race from the bear was simply the tip of this tree.

"What is this place? Where are we?"

"These are the sacred healing waters of the mountains," said Mary. "My people have come here to cleanse and to...to pray...since the beginning."

Nothing like flinging myself into someone's sacred place, thought Janey, feeling clumsy and graceless for the umpteenth time that day. But she must have dropped into this Nakoda girl's bath time for a reason. She glanced around, her eyes adjusted to the light. The cave was about three storeys high, with stalagmites and stalactites stretching long stony fingers toward each other. Behind them she caught glimpses of ledges and cubby holes scattered along the dripping walls. Below her, Mary stood waist-deep in a large pool of water, her loose shift eddying lazily around her.

"Cool," said Janey.

Mary smirked. "Now I know you are no magpie. It is a clever bird. You, you are not so clever. These waters are not cool. They are hot. That is part of their healing powers."

Yup, she had to be in the past if Mary thought *cool* only referred to temperature. But the Nakoda girl was right. The cave was steaming hot, and beads of sweat were gathering at her hairline. She needed to do something – anything – other than squat in this tree with fir needles up her butt while she melted in the heat. Climbing back out to face the bear wasn't an option. "Can I swim in the pool with you?"

Mary didn't answer right away. Janey almost asked again, thinking that the Nakoda girl had either not heard or not understood her.

"Your boots will drink up all the water," Mary said.

"If I take them off, can I come in?"

Again, a pause, as if Mary really couldn't decide. Finally, she nodded.

Janey pulled her boots off carefully, laced them together and strung them around her neck. That was the easy part. Wiggling out of her jeans on a tree limb was way harder. She bundled them with her sweater, jacket, socks and boots and clambered down.

Stepping into the hot pool made Janey gasp. She waded over to Mary and the two girls studied each other. As usual, Janey was half a head taller than the other girl, whose long dark hair dropped wet and straight to her waist.

"Put your clothes here," Mary said, beckoning her to the far side of the pool. Janey pushed through the water, feeling the heat work its way into her body, especially the parts that had banged against the fir tree on her way down. She shoved her stuff into an opening next to a bundle of soft cotton, then lowered herself into the pool.

The waters flowed around her, soothing and warm, washing away all the fear and anger and embarrassment that had clouded her day. Why should she care about a few scattered bits of popcorn and what some 16-year-old thought of her? So what if her grandmother was crushing on a Santa-wannabe? She sank gratefully under the surface, letting the hot water bubble up from a spring beneath her, swirling everything away.

Cleansed and calmed, Janey burst back into the air. "This is awesome," she called, plunging backwards to float face up in the warmth.

Mary looked puzzled. "Awesome means good? Your

English is not from here. Reverend McDougall says it means full of wonder...and fear."

"Yes, I mean good," Janey said quickly, coming to her feet. "It's good. Fabulous. Wonderful. But who's Reverend McDougall?"

"He lives on the reserve with us. He is a man of God."

"Is that how you learned English? From this reverend guy?"

"No, we have a school with a teacher. Reverend McDougall is in the church. He has great power. He helped us to...to speak with our queen. We made a treaty. When I was a child."

Despite the heat, a prickle of cold crept down Janey's back. As near as she could remember, almost all the treaties signed with First Nations people in this part of the world were created in the 1800s. That meant that when she'd stepped through that wooden hotel door, she'd time-travelled more than a century into the past. What was she doing here?

"Mary, what year are we in? What is the number? Maybe your teacher says it with the date. Or Reverend McDougall." Janey knew she sounded a bit nuts. Who asks for the year they're in?

Mary looked at her warily. Yup, she'd picked up on the crazy vibe. "It is the year of our Lord 1883," she said finally.

"Does the reverend come here too?" Janey asked, trying to move the conversation to safer ground. She ran her hand along the cave wall and discovered a trickle of cold water seeping through a crack. Cupping her hands, she gathered some coolness and tipped it over her head.

"No. He does not know this place. No white man, or girl, has come down here before. You are the first."

No wonder Mary'd taken so long to let her step into the pool. "Is this a secret place?"

"Not for my people. We come in when we pass this way. Today I gathered the red berries that grow in the meadows here. Then I saw this tree and climbed in."

"You mean, this tree isn't always here?"

Mary shook her head. "No. We tie animal skins or rope together and climb down. And up. This will be –" She stopped suddenly and held up her hand.

At first, Janey only heard the steady drip of water echoing through the cave. But as Mary grabbed her and pulled her toward a wall, she heard voices. Male voices. At least two.

"They are not my people," said Mary softly. "We must hide."

Fine with me, thought Janey, who had no intention of meeting strangers while she was dressed in nothing more than her T-shirt and underwear. She wriggled onto the ledge Mary showed her and made room for her companion.

"It stinks up here even more'n the pool down the ways. Maybe it's hell, Tom," one of the voices said.

"I ain't done nuthin' to deserve to go to hell," said another voice. "Billy, you're the one eyein' all them fine lookin' ladies in that Duluth saloon."

"I was only...jumpin' ghost of Jehosaphat!" The last bit, shouted into the cave so it echoed off the walls, was a tangle of old-fashioned words that made Janey snicker. Mary elbowed her hard in the ribs.

"Tom! Frank! Get a load of this! There's a cave down here. A secret cave, like the one that fella finds with the magic carpet."

"One of us should go down. Check it out."

"You weigh less'n us, Billy. We'll tie our rope 'round you and make sure you don't slip."

Mary's body inched closer to Janey's, forcing Janey against the back of the ledge. Over Mary's shoulder, she watched a pair of dirty leather boots descend the branches of the fir tree, followed by a body clad in an equally dirty shirt and overalls. The face, when it came into view, was bearded, but no more than 25 years old, Janey thought.

"Hey! What's it like down there?" one of the voices called from above.

"We've found ourselves another hot pool, gentlemen," Billy called up. "But this one, this one's magic."

He pulled off the rope and tied it around his clothes. "Pull the rope up. This tree's pretty steady and I'm goin' for a swim. If you're fixin' on comin' down here, leave your clothes up top." As the rope disappeared overhead, so did Billy's boots and clothing.

Janey bit the inside of her mouth to keep from giggling. But when two more sets of naked legs, followed by naked butts and backs, clambered down from overhead, she struggled to check the laughter welling up inside her. Mary must have sensed what was happening. She turned, clapped her hand over Janey's mouth and bit Janey's shoulder. Instantly the giggles disappeared, bitten off and swallowed by the girl beside her. Janey nodded to show she was under control and moved Mary's sweaty hand carefully away from her face. It was too hot to have anything else touch her.

"It's Aladdin," said the last man in.

"What's that, Frank?" asked the second man.

"It's Aladdin, the guy who found the cave with the magic carpet," Frank said.

The second fellow looked around appreciatively. Huddled next to Mary on the warm, dark ledge behind a forest of outcroppings, Janey hoped he wouldn't look too far. "It's a wonder of wonders," he said finally.

"Nope, it's our ticket to fame an' fortune," said Frank. "We've been tryin' to find gold, but this, this is the fountain of youth. People'll pay good coin to soak their bones here. We're gonna stake a claim and build ourselves a hotel right over that vent hole up there."

Janey felt Mary's body tense.

"Good idea," Tom said. "This'll be a lot easier than blastin' that railroad through these Rocky Mountains."

Wedged in behind Mary, Janey wished she could do some blasting herself, straight through Sulphur Mountain and out into some fresh air. The heat was suffocating. She wished desperately that she was somewhere else; that she'd never gone through that wooden door or even agreed to go to Banff. What was she doing here except waiting quietly until she blew up like an egg cooked too long in a microwave?

Her mind raced, looking for ways to cool down. She tried to focus on a snowstorm, imagining the cold flakes whirring around her face and skin, even as sweat crawled along her body, mixing with the water drops splashing down from the condensation above. Each drop was hotter than the next. Frantic for more space, she wriggled silently, only to be rewarded by another elbow jab from Mary.

She was going to die here, while those three guys splashed around, laughing and chattering excitedly about their plans to fence off the cave entrance and open their stupid hotel. But first, she thought grimly, they'd have to deal with her boiled, bloated body. In desperation, she began counting, hoping to make it to 100 before her head exploded and she dissolved into a hot mess of cooked body parts.

She'd reached the high 80s when Mary took her hand and pulled her off the ledge. The men had gone. Quietly they moved along the wall, past the lengthening shadows created by the stalagmites and stalactites, toward the cold trickle on the opposite side. Janey gathered as much of the cool water into her hands as she could and plunged her face into it.

"Should we pull up the tree so's no one else goes down?" one of the men outside the opening asked. Janey froze.

"Nah. It'll just be a bunch of work for no purpose. Nobody's around. Let's head to camp an' set out tomorrow to stake our claim."

As the men's voices drifted away, the girls gathered their belongings and carried them to the tree. Too hot to dress in the cave, Janey realized she would have to carry her clothes up. But she was so drained from the heat that she could barely loop her boots around her neck, let alone lift her clothes over her head. Mary reached the tree first and started up. Wearily Janey followed, each breath tied to an anchor, each arm and leg encased in concrete. Grabbing clumsily for the branch above her, she swore and pulled back her hand. The tip of a dried fir needle stuck out from under the nail of her middle finger, sending a ridiculous amount of pain pulsing through her. She forced herself not to cry. This was it, she thought – the needle in the proverbial fir tree that could break the camel's back. No. That's not how that went –

"Give me your boots," Mary commanded. Janey looked up at the outstretched hand, wondering if she could reach it. Passing her boots overhead took energy that she could barely find. "And your coat," Mary added.

The unburdening helped. Janey climbed, ignoring the throb under her fingernail, the heat rising from below, even the weight of the jeans and sweater now tied around her waist. When she finally emerged from the vent hole, she crawled to one side and collapsed onto a bed of dry leaves.

Rolling onto her back, Janey gulped the cold air and stared into the sky. Gone was the sunshine that had first greeted her that afternoon. Instead, low grey clouds were piling up like huge floating duvets, but with no promise of warmth. In fact, the temperature had plummeted. She let the chill seep into her steaming body.

"It's cool, yes?" Mary said, smiling, as she dropped Janey's boots and jacket beside her. She'd pulled on a long cotton dress, faded from many washings. "I must go. I must tell the elders about this visit from those who take only fat."

"Hey wait a second," Janey said. "I eat my vegetables."

Mary smiled. "*Wasiju* is our name for the white men – the takers of the fat," she said. "When we hunt and kill an animal, we use all of it. But your people take only the fat and the meat. The rest is left behind." She'd grown more serious. "I think those three will make problems for my people, for the Stoney Nakoda. I must go now. Those men, they want to take what is not theirs to take."

"Wait! Hang on," Janey called, sitting up to pull on her jeans and gather her thoughts. "I'm not sure...I mean, I don't know..." She didn't want to be left alone here, with a bear prowling around and the skies looking dark and foreboding. She needed a plan.

"Can I..." She tugged on her boots and laced them up. At least she'd be ready to run if that bear came back. "Can I come with you?"

Mary gazed at her. "Why are you here? Where are your people?" she asked.

My people? Janey almost laughed. She hardly had any people. There was Granny, who was off in some different century, giggling with a new boyfriend when she should be acting the way any normal grandmother did...baking cookies and, and knitting...things. And her parents? They were off on some other continent, having the time of their lives, while she was stuck here, wherever *here* was. She shrugged.

"Come then," Mary said finally. From under a nearby bush, she pulled out a Hudson's Bay blanket and an animal skin sack. She slung them over her shoulders and headed downhill.

"How do you know the bear won't come back?" Janey asked.

"The moon of the first snow is with us. Soon the bear will go underground for his winter-moons-sleep. He does not seek us."

"Then why did it chase me?" Janey asked peevishly.

"How did you meet this bear? With respect? With a greeting? Or did *Îktomnî* chase the bear to you?"

"Who's *Îktomnî*?" Janey asked, stumbling over the pronunciation.

"Our spirit man. The first Nakoda man. He makes...mischief. Sometimes."

"A trickster?"

"Yes, like that. But to see a bear is a good sign. So perhaps it was not *Îktomnî*."

Maybe *seeing* a bear is lucky, but being chased by one? Not so much. And why would she even need to be sent into a smelly cave by an even smellier bear? As she followed Mary along a ridge, questions swirled around her. Why was she time-travelling again? What was she supposed to be doing here? And how was she going to get back to –

"Heh! You can see but you do not look," Mary scolded. The Nakoda girl had stopped by some thorny bushes, and Janey, lost in thought, walked right into her.

"Sorry," Janey mumbled. "What are you..." She looked more closely. Mary was gathering bright red berries from the bushes. They were like the rose bushes that grew against Granny's garage, with the same kind of red berries that popped out in the fall. Granny had a weird name for the berries – a body part…rose feet? Rose legs? No. Rosehips! But at home they stayed on the bush all winter, a bold crimson against the snow. Who knew you could pick them and use them?

"These are for tea," Mary explained. "When the snow comes on the reserve and the wind blows cold, this tea helps us not be sick." She dropped some rosehips into her sack and continued across the slope.

"Are we going to the reserve now?"

"No. The reserve is far. And it is only good for the old and the sick ones. Or when the snow is deep." She glanced at the heavy clouds and the last of the dry leaves scurrying past in the gust of a keen, rising wind. "That will be soon."

"So where are we going now?" Even Janey could smell the sharp promise of snow. The last thing she wanted was to be caught outside in the middle of a blizzard.

"To our camp here in the mountains. Only in the moon of the mid-winter do we return to the reserve. And to the…" She drew a square with her fingers.

"School? Church? House?" Janey tried to throw in the

vocabulary, but Mary kept shaking her head and drawing more four-sided shapes in the cold air.

"Cabin? Square? Box?"

"Yes!" Mary pounced on the last word. "Box. Boxes. With four walls. To keep things in. Or keep things out. Even animals. Even people. Everywhere the takers of the fat make boxes. So many boxes with so many names – crates, chests, cabins, forts, reserves. Four sides, four walls, four fences. And now they want to make a box over the cave of our holy waters. It is not right. Look." She nodded at the mountains stretching off into the distance. "Here, we have no boxes. Here, nothing has four walls." She looked directly at Janey. "Here we are free. Always our people have lived this way."

Janey's heart sank. She turned away, unable to meet Mary's gaze. Was this why she was here? To tell this Nakoda girl that things were about to change, and not for the better? Janey had taken enough social studies classes to know that Indigenous people had been royally mistreated, their rights taken away along with their land.

Back in Edmonton, her best friend could add tons of personal details. Nicky would go all stone-faced when she told how her Cree grandmother, at the age of five, was pulled from her mother's arms and taken to a residential school. The little girl was beaten whenever she spoke her own language.

And Michael, Nicky's brother, had once shown Janey his great-uncle Nelson's tiny, childhood braids. A nun had chopped them off as soon as the little boy arrived at residential school. Nelson had snuck back and fished them out of the trash. He'd saved those braids, tied together with deer hide strips, until he gave them to Michael only days before he died.

The goal of those residential schools had been to scrub out the "Indian-ness" of the people here, to make them as white and Christian as possible. How was Janey supposed to explain all this to the sure-footed girl expertly picking her way across this mountain? How was she supposed to warn her that even though her people had always lived freely on this land, this freedom wasn't going to last?

But Mary was still talking. "We are not…not…" She paused to adjust the blanket across her shoulders for more warmth while she searched for the word. "…tillers?"

It took a moment for Janey to figure this out. "Farmers?"

"Yes. Farmers. My people are not farmers. Your people want us to…to farm on the reserve. You give us seeds for plants we do not know. We put the seeds in the reserve ground but it does not grow. The cold from the mountains comes too fast and kills the plants before we can eat them." Mary stopped again, this time to examine animal tracks beside their trail. "It is better to move freely, to follow the animals that live here."

Having spoken her piece, she straightened and moved quietly through the trees. Janey was grateful for the silence, though the wind had picked up and was whistling past her ears. A feeling of foreboding grew inside her, given what she knew about the treatment of Indigenous people. Janey sensed that Mary's freedom was about to disappear with the wind. Wondering what she should say or do, she kept her head down and allowed herself to be guided by Mary's moccasinned feet. That worked until the girl stopped and Janey nearly ran into her again.

"You will walk off a mountain if you do not learn to look," Mary said sharply, pulling off her footwear. "I do not want to swim in this water today." They'd paused, Janey realized, at the bank of a river that looked like it was one degree away from ice.

"Sorry," Janey said, and watched in dismay as Mary picked her way across, sometimes stepping thigh-deep into the water. Reluctantly Janey unlaced her boots and stuffed her socks inside them before she pulled off her jeans once again. She envied Mary, who had simply pulled the hem of her skirt up above the water until she reached the other bank, where she turned to wait.

Small grains of hail were beginning to slam sideways against Janey's face. She realized she had two choices: Die slowly of hypothermia by staying here, or die pretty well instantly by falling into the river. If she was lucky, maybe she'd drown first. Janey stepped into the water and gasped. All feeling in her feet was being swept away by the river's current. She needed to move. But when she looked up to get her bearings, she froze.

A dark-haired boy stood beside Mary and smirked at Janey. He looked to be a few years younger, but his build was stockier and the features he shared with the Nakoda girl were stretched across broader cheekbones. Mary was speaking urgently to him, and his eyes followed in the direction she was nodding, along the path she and Janey had just come from. But only for an instant. Like magnets, they pulled back to where Janey stood in her underwear, knee-deep in the river. His grin widened.

"Come!" Mary urged, waving her forward. But Janey's feet had grown too numb. If she tried to take a step, she'd stumble under the current. How was this happening to her? She looked at the riverbank behind her, wondering if she could roll herself out of the water, back to where she'd been just a few steps ago. But even that seemed too far.

"I can't," Janey wailed, as more needles of hail smacked against her face, forcing her to shut her eyes. She gave up. This was it. She was going to die of hypothermia half in and half out of this icy river. Winter would thunder in and cover her frozen form in a sheet of hail and snow and she'd stand here until the spring thaw when the birds could peck out her eyes and the bears would eat what was left of her and –

"You are…you are in a box of fear," Mary snarled, appearing in the water in front of her. "Step out!" She took Janey by the arm and tugged. "Put your foot here. Good. Now here. Yes. Here." As the sleet thickened, Janey clung to the girl's hand and blindly followed her across the river.

On the other side, the boy pulled her up the embankment and under a large pine tree where the ground was still dry. He eyed her bare legs with definite amusement. Mary cuffed him across the back of his head. "This is my silly brother. At school they call him Jonas. He has such big eyes for girls that he walks into holes," she said. Looking up from the ground where she was struggling to put on her jeans, Janey realized he was favouring his left ankle.

"Go. Tell our mother we have a guest," Mary ordered. Reluctantly Jonas left the shelter of the branches and limped into the forest.

Shaking with cold, Janey fought the laces of her hiking boots. If only she could have a little bit of the heat from earlier this afternoon. "Maybe we can go back to the hot water?" she asked, trying to control her shivering.

Mary was about to say something, but caught Janey's tiny smile. "The camp is close and it will be warm there," she said, stepping out from under the pine. Janey pulled the collar of her jacket up around her ears and followed.

By the time they found the small circle of teepees, Janey's teeth chattered uncontrollably, drowning out the wind or anything Mary shouted at her. Again the Nakoda girl grabbed her hand, pulling her past a teepee flap.

The warm, quiet darkness that greeted them almost overwhelmed Janey. While her eyes struggled to adjust, her only compass point was the glow of a fire straight ahead of her. The scent of woodsmoke drifted toward her, mingled with the odour of tanned hides and something savoury and delicious. Those stupid road snacks had been a long time ago, and Janey's stomach growled loudly in the sudden quiet. A figure by the fire chuckled and said something Janey couldn't understand.

"Come," Mary said, and gently pushed Janey toward the fire.

Janey neared, making out Jonas and an older woman. "This is my mother. Your people call her Mrs. Two Feathers," Mary said, then spoke to her mother in Nakoda.

Unsure of what to do, Janey nodded shyly at the older woman. Jonas interrupted his sister, speaking rapidly. The only word Janey could pick out was one he stumbled over. It sounded suspiciously like *bloomers*. Mrs. Two Feathers chuckled, said something else and they all laughed. Great, Janey thought. They weren't going to let her forget that she'd crossed the river in only her underwear.

"My mother thinks the little people brought you here," Jonas said. Seeing Janey's blank look, he explained. "They live inside the mountain. They are –"

"Tricksters," Mary threw in, proud of the word she'd

learned earlier that afternoon.

Unsure of what to do, Janey said nothing. Mary sat down and patted a thick fur rug beside her. Janey sank gratefully into its soft warmth and watched as Mrs. Two Feathers stirred something in a hole in the ground beside the fire. She edged closer for a better look.

The hole was lined with some sort of thick leather, its edges peeking out above the ground. The aroma of a rich, meaty stew wafted up as Mrs. Two Feathers stirred the contents inside the rawhide with a stick. Then, using the same stick, the older woman deftly rolled a large stone from the fire into the hole. The stew sizzled and bubbled, and Mrs. Two Feathers smiled.

"This is the old way of cooking," Mary said, as her mother ladled out bowls of the stew. "Your people call us the Stoney Nakoda because we cooked with hot stones."

Mrs. Two Feathers said something to Mary as she handed a bowl to Janey. "We have pots from your people to cook in," Mary added quickly. "Mostly we use them. But our mother says when the snow comes, the stones make the stew taste the best."

Janey's cold hands clutched at the bowl, grateful for its warmth, no matter how it was cooked. She sipped at the thick, fragrant broth filled with chunks of tender meat and vegetables. As the heat spread through her, her shoulders loosened and her body relaxed.

"This is wonderful," Janey said, smiling at Mrs. Two Feathers, who nodded, filled several more bowls and took them to the other side of the teepee. Only then did Janey realize that other people were gathered in the shelter.

She looked at Mary. "My grandfather," said the girl. "And

my oldest brother. His English name is Peter. He went with Jonas high into the mountains to hunt last week. They brought back a deer and four fat birds yesterday. This is the deer." She held up her bowl of stew.

Cool, thought Janey, though she didn't say anything, knowing that Mary would tease her about the stew's temperature. She took another mouthful. Granny would love this meal. If she was here, she'd probably be pestering Mrs. Two Feathers for the recipe.

Janey smiled and stretched her legs, revelling in the way the fire and the food warmed her up. Funny how she could go from almost boiling in the hot spring to almost freezing in the river in the same afternoon. Like Goldilocks, she'd finally found a place that was just right. The teepee was warm and snug. A low murmur of Nakoda drifted overhead as Mary and her family spoke to each other. Outside, the winds moaned and sheets of sleet beat against the teepee's walls. Janey's eyes grew heavy.

She was almost asleep when a man's voice, bitter and angry, pierced the comfortable warmth that had settled around her. "What's happening?" she whispered to Mary.

"My brother Peter, he does not like that your people found the sacred waters," she whispered back. "He says it will bring us…sadness."

No kidding, thought Janey.

"It will make the Nakoda people…" Mary stumbled, trying to find the word. "Like the buffalo."

Now Janey was lost. Did Mary mean they'd have to leave the mountains and roam on the plains? But the buffalo were hunted into extinc….oh.

"Disappear? Vanish?" Janey asked, waving her hand and

making the other hide her bowl behind her back.

Mary nodded. "Yes. Peter fears that our people will vanish."

He has every right to be worried, Janey thought. Was this where she was supposed to jump in and reassure them? Or warn them of what was coming? And how would that help? What on earth was she doing here?

Beside her, Jonas said something and tried to get up. But his ankle gave way and he collapsed, practically on Janey's lap. Mary snapped at him in Nakoda. In response, he rolled up his pant leg to reveal an ankle that looked puffy and sore. Janey winced in sympathy. She'd sprained an ankle during soccer practice last year. "RICE," she said out loud. The other two looked at her oddly.

"Rest, Ice, Compression and Elevation," she said, but in a lower voice. They were still looking at her as if she'd sprouted horns. "He needs to, to put his ankle higher," she said, motioning with her hands. "And he needs to tie it up. Tight. Did this happen today?"

Mary pulled a sash from the darkness, smacked her brother with it and said something in Nakoda to him. "Yes," Mary said after he responded. "When you were in the river. He was too busy looking at a new girl. He did not tie it up because he wants to look strong." She hit him with the sash again before dropping it in his lap.

"And ice. We have to apply ice... or snow," Janey said.

"To make the sash wet?" Jonas looked puzzled.

"No." Janey thought for a minute, then searched through her coat for the bag of jawbreakers. She pulled it out, dumped the candy beside Jonas and found the teepee's entrance. Scooping four large handfuls of the icy sleet and snow from outside, she stuffed them in the bag and zipped it shut before placing it carefully on the ankle.

"Now the sash doesn't have to get wet," she said, "but it would still be better if he could prop his ankle..."

Mary and Jonas were poking at the bag and rubbing their fingers in awe. Jonas grabbed one corner of the bag and lifted it to the light of the fire. He shook it and pinched it.

Brother and sister eyed her warily. "You are a trickster?"

Uh-oh. What had she done? Plastic zip bags would make no sense to them. She should never have pulled this out of her pocket. Janey reached to take it, but suddenly it was flying toward the fire. It landed against a glowing log and melted, sizzling as the snow hit the embers.

Peter stood next to the fire. He was older than Mary by at least five years, his face harder-featured and framed by braids that hung past his shoulders. He was wiping his hands as if he'd touched something nasty. "You are trouble," he said, anger hissing from him. "Leave here."

"Brother," Mary began.

"No! All the *wasiju* bring trouble. Even this one. They do not belong here. Not in this place. She must go." He stood over her, large and menacing.

"You're right," Janey said, trying to keep her voice calm. She rose to face him, taking in the flat, distrustful look in his eyes. "You don't have any reason to trust the takers of the fat. But I'm not..." What? Taking the fat? Part of the problem? It was time to leave. She shrugged on her jacket and buttoned it up, aware of the storm howling outside. "I'll go. I'll go now." She could almost feel the heat of Peter's rage, greater than that of the fire. Jonas rose to stand unsteadily beside his brother.

"Where? Where will you go?" Mary asked, bewildered. "It is cold. And dark. How will you –"

"Let her go." Heart sinking, Janey couldn't tell which brother said it, but it felt as if they both wanted to hustle her out into the cold. Even Mary looked resigned to Janey's fate.

"Listen," she said, wanting, somehow, to reach them, to warn them of a storm greater than the one blowing outside. "Your way of life? It will change. You need to watch out." She turned, all set to fling herself into the blizzard, but her boot laces were still undone and she nearly tripped over the bearskin.

Peter grabbed the sleeve of her coat. "Why? What will you do," he asked, yanking her back. Jonas put a hand on his brother's arm, as if to steady him.

Great, thought Janey, he thinks I'm the threat. Am I? "I won't do anything," she said, anger creeping in, at Peter's hostility, at her own predicament, at their future. She pulled her arm free and stooped to tie up her laces, trying to calm herself, and maybe, maybe help this family, these people who until recently had not known about the boxes and borders that would keep them in, or out. She rose again. "But if I were you, I'd get lawyers. And keep records. Write things down." She tried desperately to think of what else to say that might be useful, even as she searched for the way out into the storm.

"You know so little," Peter growled.

She turned back to face this fierce young man who sensed, more than the others, the powerful force that was about to sweep over them. "You're right. But I'm trying to learn from the past." Janey reached up and, with one finger, barely touched the deer hide strip that held together Peter's left braid. He flinched but did not move.

"This one's really important," she said. "Try, somehow, to

keep your children away from residential schools." He frowned, not understanding. What else could she say? "If you can, try to keep your children close, so they won't go to schools far away from your homes."

"Wait," Mary called. But Janey found the teepee's flap, pushed herself outside into the frigid darkness and ran. She'd never felt so useless and helpless. She wasn't Goldilocks, but a big blundering bear stumbling around blindly, away from Mary and her family, away from their future, away from the guilt of her own people. The awfulness of it all almost, almost, swept away the dread she felt when she lost her footing and slid unrelentingly down toward the thick and icy river.

CHAPTER THREE

"Here, let me help you miss," said an unfamiliar voice. "We try to make sure all the sidewalks are shovelled, but sometimes patches of ice form when the winter fairy is feeling playful."

Janey rolled over and sat up. A hand grabbed her elbow and tried to pull her to feet, but she was busy figuring out what was happening. One minute she was in a Nakoda teepee in 1883, and the next she was sprawled flat out on a concrete sidewalk in…she looked around...in sight of the Banff Springs Hotel! Yessss! But how?

"Did you break something, miss?" The voice sounded more concerned. "Miss? Should I get help?"

"No, I mean, I don't think so." Janey looked up at the bellman, the same one who'd helped them to their room. She finally took the hand he was holding out and allowed him to pull her up off the ice. She felt bruised, but not broken.

"Are you sure you're all right?" he asked as she checked herself over.

"Yes, thanks." She brushed some snow off her jeans. She needed to think.

"You're part of the Claus contingent," he went on. "I hope you're all settling in well. By the way, my name's Sam. Sam McAuley."

"Thanks for the help, Sam, but I've gotta go." Janey desperately wanted to find the door she'd come through, the one that had taken her into the past. Because she really had gone into the past, hadn't she? She just needed to find the door that had led her there. But as she hurried along the sidewalk, all she could see was a flat, fieldstone wall, with not a door in sight.

"Janey!" Oh c'mon. She'd told Sam she was fine. That bellhop needed a life. Maybe the door was around the corner?

"Janey!"

"What?!" She spun around, ready to tell Sam to mind his own business. But the bellhop had vanished. Instead, Max's tall, lean form loped down the path toward her.

Where was a good wooden door with an escape into the past when you needed it? Janey watched warily as Max approached, hunched forward, hands shoved into the pockets of his jacket, his face scrunched against the cold. At least it wasn't full of the disapproval she'd last seen on him.

"The Olds want to know if you will go to the museum," he said when he reached her.

What was he saying? "The olds? What do you mean?" She could feel a bruise starting up on her knee.

Something buzzed and Max scrambled to pull out his phone. Was she this bad when she'd had hers?

He checked it, stuffed it back in his pocket and looked up. "They want to know if you –"

"Do you mean Granny and Charlie?"

"Yes. The Olds. *Die Alten.*"

Ah. This was beginning to make sense. But Janey didn't want to go to a museum; she wanted to find the portal that had led her into the past. She flexed her bruised knee and put her weight on it.

Max stepped in front of her. "Look. Stop for a moment. Can we begin again?"

Janey sighed, realizing she wouldn't find that door today. He frowned. "Yes," she said quickly. "But I'm all out of caramel corn and chocolate balls." They smiled at each other for an instant, before Janey shivered. "I need to get inside," she said. What she really needed, she decided as they pushed through the hotel's main revolving door, was a shower and a change of clothes.

"I am...I was...worried," Max said, as they walked through the lobby.

"About me?"

"No!"

Well, that was definite. "About how the Olds are acting?"

He considered for a moment, then allowed another smile to cross his lips. "That's just Grandfather. He was trying to make people feel...better."

Before Janey could ask what they needed to feel better about, the elevator doors slid open. They waited as a family with two little girls filed out. "He is *so* coming, isn't he, Daddy," said the younger one. She might have been four.

"Absolutely, Ruby. Santa knows we're here and he'll know if you and Eva are being good or bad," said the father. As the elevator door closed, Janey caught Ruby sticking out her tongue at Eva from behind her father's back.

Several floors passed in silence before Max cleared his throat. "Do you like the pin?"

Janey started. She'd been miles – or floors – away, dreaming of a hot shower. "What pin?" The elevator stopped to let in an older couple.

"The pin. The pin I gave you. It's old, you know. My family has had it for a long time." He caught her blank look. "Did you lose it?"

"I don't know what you're talking about."

He sighed, exasperated. "Before you rushed out and told no one where you were going and made your grandmother worry, I gave you a small box. Don't you remember?"

That box! Was it still in her pocket? She shoved her hand into her jacket and pulled out the tiny wooden container. It was a wonder it had survived her dive down the fir tree, not to mention that last tumble. She waved it at him. "See, I didn't lose it," she said. "Is Granny really worried?" She pried open the lid.

As the couple stepped out at the next floor, Max shrugged. "She said you probably needed fresh air. Do you like it?"

A small silver pin glinted in the light. Twisted strands of silver formed a circle around silver mountains and a trio of green enamel fir trees. The word *Banff* ran across the bottom in raised letters.

"When Grandfather said I should come here, I remembered about this pin. My father gave it to me a few years ago, but I think it's for a girl. So I brought it. Grandfather said it would be nice for you."

She turned it over. *Remember* was engraved across the back. Remember what?

She raised an eyebrow at Max and he shrugged. "I don't know what it means. My father doesn't either. I mean, I know what *remember* means. But not why it's there. I guess we have forgotten to remember."

"Thank you. It's lovely." She closed the box, catching the sore fingernail on the clasp. She swore softly and inspected the fir needle under her throbbing nail. In fact, everything ached. When the elevator door opened, she hurried to their suite, ready to find her bedroom and dive into the shower.

"Good. There you are," Granny said. She and Charlie were sitting on the couch. Were they still holding hands?

"Glad you're both back. We were wondering if you want to see a bit of Banff before we order up dinner. Maybe visit the Cave and Basin museum? Max likes history and Charlie hasn't been able to take him. I could drive you two over."

"The thing is, Janey," Charlie cut in, "it's risky for us all to go out together. At least not until after Christmas."

Can no one speak in plain English, Janey wondered. Nothing was making any sense today. She took a breath.

"I'm sorry, Charlie, but why can't we all go out together? And what does Christmas have to do with it?" And where was the bedroom she and Granny shared?

"At this time of year, a big guy with a white beard really attracts attention, even in civvies," Charlie said. "Unless I'm at an event, I try not to wander around town until after Christmas, when I trim my beard and avoid wearing red. I don't want kids being confused about seeing me in jeans and a sweatshirt one minute, and in the Santa suit the next. Destroys the magic. So I stay in. But that's why it's so nice that you're all here with me."

Janey caught his glance at Granny and tried not to roll her eyes.

"But you guys should go out and see the world, or at least explore Banff."

If only he knew how much I've already seen, thought Janey. "I'm sorry, Charlie, but not tonight. I'm really whacked, and I don't feel like going out anywhere," she said. "It was a long drive down." She shivered again. "And I really need a hot shower."

A phone went off in what she now knew was the boys' bedroom. No way would Janey ever step in there again. But it seemed to her that as the phone rang, the others all froze.

Only with the fourth jangling set of trills did Max and Charlie dash into their bedroom. Weird.

Janey pointed to a door on the other side of the room. "Is this our room?"

Granny nodded and followed. "You're not coming down with something, are you?"

Janey shook her head. "I don't think so. Let me shower and I'll feel better."

"The thing is," Granny said, then hesitated. She shut their bedroom door. "The thing is, kiddo, I was kind of hoping you'd keep Max company while he's here, and not go off on your own too much."

This time Janey did roll her eyes. "You promised no babysitting," she said, pulling off her jacket and throwing it on her bed. She placed the box with the pin beside it.

"It's true, I did, and he's big enough to look after himself, but he's going through a lot at the moment."

"Like what?"

Granny frowned. "It's not my place to say. But Max is here by himself, and it would be a help if you hung out with him. Took his mind off things."

"He's hard to get a handle on. And is he glued to that phone? I promise, if I ever get another one, not to check it every 30 seconds."

Granny pursed her lips. "Like I said, he's dealing with a lot and everything's twice as hard in another language. But he tries. He chatted with me for a long time before I sent him to find you. Nice kid. Like your Michael."

"He's not *my* Michael," Janey cut in quickly.

"I'd bet he was starting to think you were his before he left for hockey school last August," Granny said. "I saw the way he was looking at you at the going-away barbecue."

"Yeah, but I saw the way he looked when Maggie walked in." Maggie lived down the street and was a grade behind them.

Janey sometimes wished people had flashing buttons they could press so other people would know if they were interested in them. It would make things so much easier. When Michael showed up for every one of her soccer games, she figured it was just school spirit. Nicky said something once about Michael crushing on a soccer player. Maggie was on the team. And then Michael raved about a camping trip where he ran into Maggie and her family on a hike.

Granny clucked her tongue. "He was smiling at Nicky, who was coming in behind Maggie with a stack of hamburgers."

The last thing Janey wanted, after her trip into the past – if that had really happened – was to discuss her nonexistent love life. "Can we talk about something else? And have you seen my toiletry kit?" Janey opened her suitcase on the bed and rooted through it.

Granny pulled the bag from Janey's backpack and dropped it in front of her before sitting on the bed. She found the box with the pin and opened it. "Now this is pretty."

"Max isn't sure what the *Remember* on the back refers to," Janey said.

Granny took out the pin and turned it over. "More's the pity," she said. "What we forget we're doomed to repeat."

Janey looked at her oddly. "Your grampa used to say that," said Granny, her voice softening, lost in her own memories.

"Speaking of Grampa, did he, or you, ever live here in Banff? Or in the Rockies?" If she had some family history here, it could be a clue for why she had travelled into the past.

Granny shook her head. "No, we were Hudson's Bay Company people from way back, but not down here. Your grandpa and I honeymooned out here. Four short days in a canvas tent. Lovely times, but we never lived here."

A light tap ended the conversation. Janey opened the door to find Max standing there, looking oddly flushed.

"Grandfather says we should eat and then go to the movies," he announced.

"What a great idea," Granny said. "I think *It's a Wonderful Life* is on tonight. You love that movie, Janey. We'll order room service early so you can get a good seat."

"But I really, really don't want to go out again," Janey said in a low voice.

"Don't worry. The movies are right here at the hotel. And there's free popcorn!" Granny looked meaningfully at her granddaughter.

Janey glared at her for a moment, then grinned. "You know, I can see right through you, right to your back-collar button...trying to get rid of me, huh?"

"I do not wear collar buttons, kiddo." Granny was smiling. "I take it that's a yes. I think I saw a pizza menu in that drawer by the fridge. See if you can find it, Max."

He nodded and left. "You should come too, Granny."

"Nah. I'll stay here and keep Charlie company. Maybe I'll teach him how to play double rummy."

"Are you going to teach him how to cheat too?"

"What! *Moi?*" Granny grinned and left the room.

Max had never seen *It's a Wonderful Life*. He couldn't understand why Janey and her family watched it every December.

"It's a classic," Janey said, as they left the impromptu theatre and wandered back through the festive lobby which smelled of pine and cinnamon and…Christmas. The strains of "Joy to the World" floated softly from the speakers. Through the small glass panes of the bronze revolving door, snowflakes drifted gently past the courtyard lights. She hugged herself, barely able to restrain her delight. Soon her parents would be back and they'd all be able to celebrate together. And everything would be back to normal. In fact, after the hot shower and the holiday movie, everything *was* normal. Even Max was behaving sort of normally. Maybe whatever she thought had happened earlier this afternoon had really been a way to escape from that disastrous first meeting.

"He lets that Potter man take all their money," Max grumbled. Janey glanced at him. Was he really going to dissect the movie and kill its magic? But a hint of a smile played on his face as he looked at her. Max might not be such a bore to have around, she thought. Maybe Granny was right. He needed someone to show him how to have a little holiday fun.

They turned from the lobby into a passageway just as a jazzy version of "Let It Snow" came on. She began snapping her fingers to the rhythm, and then, since no one but Max was anywhere nearby, she did a few of the old-fashioned dance moves from the movie.

Max stopped to lean against a wall and study her, arms crossed in front of him. He was still smiling, but one eyebrow had climbed to about the height of the speaker hanging from the ceiling. She didn't care if he was laughing at her. It was almost Christmas!

"Stop being such a…party pooper," she said, shimmying up to him in the empty passageway. *"Just dance with her one time and you'll give her the thrill of her life,"* she said, quoting the movie before stepping back and twirling. What did she care anyway? She was –

His arm shot out and grabbed her hand, pulling Janey toward him, while his other hand pushed her away. She was spinning with the beat, being pulled back and away and back again, kept from falling only by the firm hold of Max's hand.

"Hey, you're good," she said, before he sent her twirling again.

"So are you. But only one of us can lead, and that should be me." Was he really smiling? Did it matter? She stopped thinking and let the music flow.

The song ended as he pulled her close and dipped her effortlessly in the darkened hallway. For a moment, her world was upside down.

In the distance, someone clapped. Max pulled her back up as Sam the bellman drifted toward them.

"Nice moves, you guys." Janey and Max jumped apart. What just happened? Sam passed between them, looking straight ahead. "I'd advise you not to go waltzing off a landing and tumbling down any steps like our resident ghost. She tripped down those stairs over there on her wedding day and broke her neck. Apparently, she haunts the hotel to this very day."

Long after Sam disappeared down the passageway, the bridal ghost seemed to linger between them. What to say?

What to do? Janey tried desperately to think of what they were talking about before she'd lost her mind and started to dance. Christmas...the movie...the bad guy Potter taking all of good guy George Bailey's money...

"Besides," she said, as if nothing had interrupted them, "George doesn't let him take the money. Potter steals it. And everyone around George, the whole town, helps him replace the money, because he's such a good guy."

"What?" It was Max's turn to look confused.

"In the movie. The one we just watched."

Max stared at her for what seemed like forever, his confusion slowly disappearing. But in its place, that look of superiority – or was it bitterness? – settled on him like a bad smell.

"But I want the bad guy to be punished," Max said fiercely. "For once, just once, the police should catch the criminals and punish them. Put them in jail and...and... throw away the lock. That would be wonderful."

Janey was confused. "The key?"

"The key? The key...thing...is that bad people can get away with...bad things."

"No, I meant –" Janey shook her head. "I think it's better to look at the good. If you're a good person, if you try to do the right thing, you're rewarded, like in that movie."

"Not always," Max muttered. "Good is hard. Being a good person can make you a target for evil."

Bewildered, Janey watched him storm up the stairway and disappear down a long hall. She wasn't sure what had just happened, but she didn't have the energy to try and fix it. Instead, she wandered through the hotel, exploring the nooks and balconies that popped up in unexpected places. She nearly tripped over a young boy sprawled on a staircase, studying the stone steps.

"Don't walk on it!" he called out. Puzzled, Janey moved back. "You're not an *it*," she said, crouching down beside him.

"Not me! The fossil. Look, it's right here. And here's another one," he said excitedly, his small flashlight bouncing around the staircase. Janey looked more closely. Sure enough, a ghostly, bone-white piece of lace the size of a man's thumb glowed from the stone step. "It's from about a million years ago, and here it is, trapped in this stone, where hundreds of people a day can walk by."

"Or crouch down and stare at it," Janey said. "It's pretty cool."

"There's more up here. I've lost my sister but I found these instead."

"Shouldn't you be finding your sister?"

He shrugged. "I think Lily went to count the jellybeans in the jar. For the contest. But she takes forever. She's only six." He stood up. "I can show you a painting of the guy who built this hotel. He signed it backwards. That's because they accidentally built the hotel backwards. They gave the best views of the lake to the workers. But then the hotel burned down and now it's not backwards anymore. Do you want to see it? The painting, I mean. My name's Ben."

"Wow. Hi Ben. Sure. And I'm Janey." The boy was a verbal search engine, full of information she didn't even know she needed. But his cheeriness was way easier to handle than Max's unpredictable grouchiness. She followed Ben up the stairs and along a gallery. One side was lined with bits of old furniture, while the other had archways that looked down into a gorgeous, chandeliered room complete with lances, a suit of armour and lots of wrought-iron grill work.

"Lily thinks this is the ballroom for the king and queen of the hotel," Ben said. "But I've seen an even better one. I just can't find it again."

"Sounds like you need to keep better track of stuff. First you lose your sister and now the ballroom."

"I'll find 'em again. I'm not worried. And look. Here's the picture. See this signature? ENROH NAV 1903."

"Who's that? I thought this was supposed to be a picture of someone." Janey stared at the dark autumn forest scene with the odd name in the left corner.

"No. It's *by* someone. He signed his name. Read it backwards," Ben commanded.

"Van Horne! You're right."

"Course I am. Now I better find Lily. She can be such a pain."

Janey, who'd never had a brother or sister, hoped he'd be successful.

"The pin looks good on you, Janey," Charlie said the next morning as she joined the other three for breakfast. The room service trolley held a stack of pancakes higher than the coffee pot, as well as scrambled eggs, sausages and a basket of cranberry muffins.

"Thanks," Janey said, plopping several pancakes on her plate. Before she left her room, she'd debated about wearing pin. But it might make up for whatever she'd said last night that made Max storm away. She tried to catch his eye.

"And Max, it was thoughtful of you to bring it." She

fingered the pin on the neckline of her sweater. "So... thanks."

Max didn't answer. He was staring at her breakfast, scowling. "What's wrong?" she asked. "There's more pancakes on the trolley. Should I pass you some?"

"Those are big, fat things, not like the *Palatschinken* we have at home," he said. "And where is the marmalade?"

"Blech. Marmalade on pancakes? That's disgusting," Janey shot back. Why did she even try to be nice?

"Hold it, you guys. Time out," Charlie said, forming a T with his hands. "Janey, where Max comes from, marmalade is any kind of jam, and not just the orange stuff. And Max, these are fat because they're light and airy to soak up all of our famous maple syrup."

With a flourish, Charlie slid a pancake onto his grandson's plate and poured out some syrup from a small silver pitcher. "Try them together," he urged, adding jovially, "your mother loved maple syrup." Was it Janey's imagination, or did Charlie's smile disappear as he set the pitcher back down?

Max said nothing, but finally cut one small piece of pancake and put it in his mouth. Janey watched, fascinated. In the time it took for him to chew that one forkful, Janey could have done a lap around the room. "Yes," Max said finally. "I remember." Then he pushed back from the table and left the room, nearly knocking over the small Christmas tree in the hallway.

"Well," said Granny, pouring herself a cup of coffee. "If you guys want to have a dip in the actual hot springs after you've been to the museum, I'll drop you there and pick you up an hour or two later."

What just happened? Did no one else think it was weird

the way Max left the table? If he wasn't fond of whatever we put on our pancakes, he could have said so. Janey stabbed a breakfast sausage and bit into it ferociously.

"Those hot springs are the reason why we're here today," Charlie said, as if nothing had happened.

"I thought we were here today because you look so good in a red suit," Granny said. "Which reminds me," she turned to Janey. "Pack your bathing suit. I know they rent them at the Upper Hot Springs, but trust me, you'd rather wear your own. You too, Max."

Max had returned, and as he slid into his chair, Charlie looked at him quizzically. Max shook his head.

"You know this, right?" Charlie asked. "About why we have this big park here in the Rocky Mountains?"

"Yes." Max seemed to be pulling himself together. "You told me about this when we drove here from the airport. Three railroad workers discovered hot springs here in 1883 and –"

"Those guys didn't discover the hot springs," Janey cut in. "The Stoney Nakoda people had been using those waters for...forever." The image of those naked, hairy men clambering down into the cave dangled before her. She smiled. Max scowled.

Granny cleared her throat and put a gentle hand on Max's. "The Stoney Nakoda are one of the First Nations here, Max."

"In German we call them *Indianer*," Max said.

"Yeah, but not here," said Janey. "Now we say *Indigenous*. But you can break that down, just like *European* breaks down into different nations." For once Janey felt she could teach Max something.

"Names can change," Charlie said. "Sometimes history changes names, sometimes people realize old names make no sense or sound insulting. Wars change names, or at least the winners of the wars can change the names of the losers. And sometimes names change for good reasons, like a marriage."

Janey looked up sharply. "It doesn't have to," she snapped. "My mum has the same name she was born with." Was he thinking about Granny with that last bit?

Granny dropped her coffee cup into her saucer a bit louder than usual. "I could get used to being served every meal with fine china and cloth napkins," she said, obviously unwilling to discuss the topic of changing names. "But enough lollygagging. Charlie, you probably need to get ready for Santa's brunch." She pushed back from the table and looked at Janey and Max. "I'll be ready to go in ten minutes. The last one out the door is a rotten egg."

Max glanced warily at the last bit of his scrambled egg. "What...why?"

"It's an expression Max," Charlie said. "Eat up and don't dawdle, or you'll miss your first ride in Marilyn. I'll call and make sure she's waiting when you get down there. No. I'm not explaining any more. You'll see."

Janey smiled at Max's mystified expression. But when they stepped out of the hotel and the bellman opened the door to Granny's bright yellow Cadillac, Janey had to laugh. Max looked like a little boy who'd been handed a fabulous new toy.

"You mean, this is yours? We can ride in this?" he asked.

"Hop in," said Granny. "Me and Marilyn have been around the block a few times, but we're holding it together," she said, adding, "I call her Marilyn on account of the colour." The puzzled look returned to Max's face.

"Marilyn Monroe's a famous blond movie star from a long time ago," Janey explained.

"Not that long ago," Granny said curtly before stepping on the gas. Janey was grateful Granny had decided to keep the top up in the frigid weather. Her grandmother loved showing off her convertible. Max responded enthusiastically, asking lots of questions about how Granny had rescued the old car and refinished it.

A faint whiff of rotten eggs greeted them in the museum's parking lot, and Janey felt the skin on the back of her neck prickle. She'd been trying not to think about what had – or hadn't – happened yesterday. The sane, rational part of her was saying she'd slipped on some ice outside the hotel and had a brief, vivid daydream, or even a concussion.

But this stink of rotten eggs? Even her body remembered it, what with the goosebumps marching up and down her arms. That throbbing under her fingernail was real too. And last night, after her shower, she'd noticed a bite mark on her shoulder, huge and red, exactly where Mary had bitten her in the pool. It had to be real.

Granny stopped to take a deep breath. "Some might say this is the stink of hell, but this sulphur was the smell of money back in the day."

"You mean this rotten-egg stink is sulphur?" Janey asked.

"They don't call it Sulphur Mountain for nothing."

The smell was stronger when they walked into the cave through a tunnel, obviously built later so people wouldn't have to climb down a fir tree. How weird, Janey thought, seeing what time and tourists had done to the massive cavern. The stalagmites and stalactites had disappeared, chipped away by construction workers or souvenir hunters over more than a century. She could sort of see where she and Mary had splashed about, but part of it was covered with the viewing platform she was standing on. These days, visitors couldn't even stick their fingers into the pool because endangered snails lived there.

Despite the cooler air from the tunnel, Janey felt as if the heat and the smell were closing in, just as they had when she was on the ledge behind Mary. She pushed her way past the exhibits and back into the fresh, cold, outside air.

"Was it the heat or the smell of the sulphur?" Max asked when he joined her a few minutes later.

"Both, I think."

"For me too," he said, and added quickly, "but I liked the museum."

They walked along in a silence that seemed...almost friendly, she thought. Maybe Marilyn had done the trick. They climbed some stairs to the top of the museum and followed a path to the vent hole, now fenced off and grated, sending clouds of steam into the winter air. Had she really slid into that? She looked up the snow-covered hill. At least no bears lurked anywhere nearby.

Companionably they drifted back down, past the arches of an old pool and along a path toward a small building. *Enemy Aliens, Prisoners of War, 1914-1920*, said the sign beside the door. A fierce wind had sprung up and, eager to step out of its way, they pushed into the building.

"Look, some of this is in German," Max said, studying the posters and pictures on the walls. "What does *internment* mean?"

Janey thought about it. She'd learned about people with Japanese backgrounds herded into camps during the Second

World War, even those who were born in Canada. If their parents or their grandparents had come from Japan, they were suddenly enemy aliens without any rights, shipped off to internment camps. But she'd never heard about camps like this in the First World War.

"It means keeping people in a…in a kind of a prison," Janey said.

"But, these are Austrians. And Hungarians. Look. These are people...people...like me," Max said.

"Well, I think they were mostly Ukrainians," Janey said, scanning the display. "They were part of the Austro-Hungarian Empire back then. And that's who we were at war with. Austrians and Hungarians and Ukrainians and whatever else that empire covered."

Max moved from display to display, and Janey could tell he was becoming upset. "Maybe we should go find Granny," she suggested, heading back to the door.

"Only 10 years earlier you wanted us here," Max said, as if he hadn't heard her. He was reading some immigration posters from the early 1900s. "It's all in German, telling us how nice it is here. And then, a decade later, you put these people, whole families, in prison because they came from somewhere else."

"Hang on a min –"

Max cut her off, his voice rising. "These weren't even prisons. You made them work. Look. It says the prisoners had to build the highway from Banff. And bridges. And they had to clear recreation grounds. For what? So you 'real Canadians' could play golf? This is forced labour. It's one step away from human trafficking. Your country is...is...horrible."

Janey bristled. "Wait a second, buddy. At least we didn't

put people in concentration camps."

"Concentration camps, internment camps, what's the difference?" Max shot back.

"The difference is that we didn't kill people because they were Jewish, or handicapped, or gay," Janey said.

Max opened his mouth to say something, closed it grimly and left.

Janey fumed. That went well. How dare Max say those things? She wanted to chase him down and, and…shake him. What was wrong with him? How was she supposed to spend another three days with this jerk?

She pulled open the door, determined to find Granny and beg to be allowed to go home. Janey could take the bus back to Edmonton and Granny could stay in Banff with Charlie, if that's what she wanted. Janey would crash with Nicky, at least until Michael returned to Edmonton.

Careful not to run into Max, Janey walked back along the trail that led up the hill. She found Granny on a platform at the top, level with the vent hole. Despite the frigid weather, a small waterfall tumbled under the walkway, heated by the hot springs. So beautiful, Janey thought. But so stinky.

"Imagine climbing down through that to have a hot bath," Granny said, nodding at the grate.

"My imagination's pretty good."

"I'm sure it is," Granny said, smiling. "Now, what have you done with Max?"

"I think…we…umm…we had a difference of opinion," Janey said. "No, it wasn't even that. It was more –"

"Aw, c 'mon kiddo. Really? For the love of Pete. Is it too much to ask that you go easy on him?"

Janey blanched. Her grandmother sounded really upset.

Maybe going back to Edmonton was the best thing for everyone.

"Granny, I could catch –"

"– Max before he disappears down into one of these hidden caves?" Granny cut in. She sighed, tucked her arm into Janey's and steered her down to the parking lot. "Let's go find him."

He was waiting by the Cadillac, kicking viciously at the piles of snow along the edge of the pavement. Charlie had suggested Max leave his cell phone behind this morning. He was probably suffering from withdrawal, Janey thought spitefully.

"Time for the Upper Hot Springs?" Granny asked cheerily. "It's only a few minutes away. You guys can drown your troubles. Or each other, from the looks of it."

As if on cue, they both shook their heads. "I would prefer the pool at the hotel," Max said, careful to avoid looking at Janey.

"And I've...I've got some reading to do," Janey muttered.

"Oh, for the love of Pete," Granny said again. "All right. Get in. We'll head back."

Max disappeared up the stairs to the second floor of the lobby as soon as they arrived at the hotel.

"Go fix this," Granny said, watching his retreating form.

Janey said nothing. She wasn't even sure what she'd done wrong.

"Please." Granny squeezed her arm. "I can't say much, but I know he's going through a lot."

Janey sighed. "The things I do for you," she said, before dragging herself up the grand staircase. On the second floor, hallways veered left and right, spilling into restaurants, reading areas, bars and balconies. She had no clue about where to start looking.

A little girl in a red velveteen dress was pushing an old chair across the hall. "Lily, stop that. You're not allowed." Ben shoved the chair back against the wall.

"But I want to see the squirrel." Lily ran up to the stone creature that decorated a railing. "Look. It's eating something. What's it eating?" Her brother sighed, exasperated, but hoisted the little girl up so she could see properly.

"I was only a little bit older than that when my mother died," a voice behind her said. Janey turned. Max was sitting in a wingback chair against the other wall, shoulders hunched forward.

"The girl or the boy?" Janey asked.

"The boy. I was eight."

"I'm so sorry," Janey said. "That must have been awful for you." It sounded lame, but what else could she say? They stood there for a while, watching Lily pat the stone squirrel.

"Was she sick?" Janey finally asked.

"Yes."

"So," she asked after a pause, "how does a kid from Austria have a Canadian grandfather?"

"My mum was Charlie's daughter. She was travelling in Europe when she met my father in Vienna. She was supposed to go on, further east, all the way to China, but she stayed." He paused before adding: "She loved maple syrup. I can barely stand to smell it now."

Huh. The scene at breakfast made sense, Janey thought. "Sounds like your mum and mine both love – loved – to travel," she said. He was still looking at the little girl. "Look, I'm sorry for what I said earlier at the museum. It all happened a long time ago and –"

"No. It's still happening today," Max said, pushing himself up from the chair. "We still have hundreds of ways to take away people's freedom. For no reason. Or because some criminal can make lots of money. Look at the ones who steal people from poor countries. Human traffickers sell them and lock them in illegal factories; or if you're a woman, in places for sex. It's like they're in jail, with no hope. Look at your Indigenous –"

"Hold on a minute here. We don't lock them..." Her words, which had grown louder, dropped away as her thoughts grew more tangled. Nicky was always going on about how unfairly Indigenous people were treated and how often they were jailed compared to…everyone else. But this wasn't about…aagghhh! She needed to think.

Janey walked away, confused and angry. She'd promised her grandmother to fix things, but she was only making it worse. Since she and Max couldn't get along, the only thing she could do was to put distance between them.

But Max wasn't finished. He followed her, flinging awful facts at her like hard little rocks. Why was he so angry? How was this her fault?

"We build fences and walls all the time to keep people in, and out," he went on. "Your country turned away a boat full of Jews during the Second World War because you didn't want them here."

"I just told you that this all happened in the past," Janey snapped. She wished she could shake him off before she said something she'd regret. Why was he still following her? "Would you leave me alone," she hissed as he put a hand on her arm.

"Listen for one minute," he begged.

Forget it, Janey thought. She pushed open another door, hoping to put it between them, but he squeezed through with her.

"You need to know –" He stopped.

The door behind them clanged shut. And disappeared. So did the hotel. Once again Janey was standing in the middle of a forest. But this time it was sloppy with melting snow. And Max was right beside her.

CHAPTER FOUR

Janey spun toward Max. "You've actually followed me here? Really? All I wanted was to get away from you. But you've even followed me here! What is your problem? Go away!"

Max looked stunned. He took a wary step back, as if from a dangerous animal that might attack if he moved too quickly. It reminded Janey of the bear, and she scanned their surroundings. She was sure they'd travelled back into the past. But was it the same place? Was the bear still around? Was she going to land in that cave again? She raised her head and sniffed. Not the faintest whiff of rancid fat. Or sulphur. Just fresh mountain air, warmed by soft sunshine. High overhead, an eagle drifted gently in the wind.

"Where are we?" Max asked softly. He was turning slowly, taking in the fir trees, the naked aspens and the enormous wall of a mountain that loomed behind them. "This is not Banff. Are you...? Did we...?" He narrowed his eyes as he looked at her again. "Did you put drugs in those pancakes?"

"No! How could you even say something like that? You are just the biggest frigging pain in the butt. No wonder you have to spend Christmas here. I'll bet nobody back home wants to spend it with you."

As furious as she was, Janey realized that the words she'd just spat from her mouth were ones she should have swallowed. Her vicious little balls of spite stopped Max in his tracks. His face, pale and grim, dulled his eyes to the colour of slate.

"I'm sorry," she said quickly. "I shouldn't have said that." For the umpteenth time, Janey wondered when she'd learn to think before she said something. Max looked like he was in pain.

She touched his arm gently, trying to remember how she'd felt the first time she'd landed in the past, several summers ago. She'd been confused, scared and...alone. At least Max didn't have to face this on his own.

"I'm pretty sure we're still in Banff National Park," she said, then looked around again. "Although we're not anywhere near the town site. I don't recognize that mountain there at all. Do you?"

Max shook his head. "But how...? Where...? Why...?" His voice trailed off in the middle of each question.

"We're in the past," Janey said matter-of-factly. She watched his face as it processed what she was saying. First the doubt – had he heard right? Janey nodded. Then the disbelief. No way, he was thinking. Janey nodded again.

"Are you...are you just a little bit crazy?" he finally asked.

Janey grabbed Max and spun him around. "Take a look, Max. No hotel, no roads, no street lights, no nothing." They stood there, two young people lost in a vast wilderness, until a faint beat, like drops of water hitting the bottom of an empty bucket, caught their attention.

"An axe," Max said, looking in the direction of the sound. "Someone is chopping wood. We can't be too far from...from somewhere."

"Don't get your hopes up," Janey said. "And we are somewhere. I'm just not sure where, exactly. Or when." She started toward the thwack-thwack of the axe. Max put his hand on her arm again.

"Would you stop doing that," she said, smacking his hand away. "Your grabbing me is probably why you're here in the first place."

"What do you mean, when?" He sounded desperate. "What did you mean about being in the past?"

"I sometimes go back in time," Janey said. It was the first time she'd ever said this out loud, let alone to someone else. She watched to see how Max reacted. "But this is the first time someone else has come with me."

"But how? How do you go back?" Behind him, a second eagle joined the first, their broad wingspans stitching invisible seams into the eggshell blue of the sky.

"I don't know," she said finally. "You saw how it happened. I didn't mean to go back but then I went through a door and here...I...am." She slowed. Both times she'd gone through a door at the hotel. Was it the same door? She couldn't be sure. She'd been so upset both times that she'd blindly pushed open whatever door was in her way. "Do you remember the door we came through?"

Max shook his head. "And if this is the past, how do you go back to the present. To our time?"

"Ah. The million-dollar question." She remembered sliding down the embankment in the snowstorm yesterday. "I'm not sure. It just happens."

"And why? Why do you come here, into this past?"

She shrugged. When she'd time-travelled a couple of years before, someone told her that she had to stop something bad from happening. She had no clue what her mission might be now. "I don't know, Max," Janey said finally. "Let's find out what we can about what's going on here, and then maybe that will tell us why we're here."

Silently, they picked their way through wet, mud-coloured leaves that covered cleverly hidden patches of ice and slush, until Max thought of another question. "When was the last time you did this?"

This was one question she could answer. "Yesterday. After we first met. After I left the suite." She was trying to gauge the season. Was it spring or fall? She'd met Mary right before a winter storm. Was it the same time? Would she meet Mary again?

"It was an interesting meeting," Max said. As he glanced at her, he pressed his lips together, trying not to smile. "I have never seen such a performance."

In spite of herself, Janey chuckled. "Yeah, if I have to make an entrance, it should be one to remember." In the distance, someone called out, followed by a thundering crash as something toppled over.

"I think we're heading toward a lumberjack camp," Janey said. "This'll be a real Canadian experience for you."

They made their way through the trees along a large, wide valley, flanked on one side by the massive mountain wall, topped by stadium-sized outcroppings that looked like giant teeth or castle ramparts. The sky was empty now, the eagles carried away by the gentle wind under their wings. It felt like spring, Janey realized, as if the area was thawing and readying itself for warm weather, instead of hunkering down to prepare for winter. But the occasional pocket of cold that rose from the ground made her tug her knit hat from her coat pocket, pull it down around her ears and tuck her hair underneath.

"Halt. I swear if ya don't stop, I'll shoot ya."

Max and Janey froze. Was the voice shouting at them? The valley suddenly grew quiet, axes, birds, even the wind stilled by the command. Someone screamed and they jumped.

When the shot rang out, Max grabbed Janey's arm and yanked her down onto the forest floor with him. His fast, rasping breaths kept time with her own nervous gasps of air. Someone was stumbling and crashing through the bushes not too far away, and a new, fearful panting wove into the sound of their own breathing.

"I told ya, I'm gonna shoot ya dead if ya don't stop," the same voice called again. The warning only spurred the runner on, closer toward them.

Max brought his mouth next to Janey's ear. "We should move," he whispered. But even as Janey nodded and started up, a thin, bearded man burst through the bushes and tripped over them. Janey and Max rolled away from each other as the man landed on his hands and knees. Silently, he put a finger to his lips, rose to a crouch and dashed off behind them.

Janey stood to follow him, but a bullet whizzed past. She crumpled back onto the ground and huddled against Max. She could still hear the man retreating behind her, which meant he hadn't been shot. If she and Max lay here quietly, maybe things would settle down and they could sneak away.

But just as she raised her head to check out the landscape, a pair of black boots broke through the brush and stopped at their heads. Janey glanced up. Although the figure was backlit by the sun, she could make out a dull brownish-yellow uniform and a rifle aimed at them.

"What the...? Wait a minute... Did you guys see a –"

"That way," Janey and Max both said, as if they'd rehearsed it. Problem was, they hadn't rehearsed the direction. Janey pointed one way, and Max the opposite, like some old cartoon version of a chase. Neither direction was where the fleeing man had gone.

"Get up!" In case they hadn't understood the order, the rifle poking hard at their jackets made it clear. This was a soldier who didn't think their cartoon response was funny. "Identify yourselves."

"Okay, okay," Janey said, trying to think as she rose to her feet. Despite diving for cover, her hair was still tucked under her tuque. Could she pass herself off as a boy? What year was she in? Would it be less dangerous if she said she was a girl, even though she was dressed in jeans?

The soldier was shorter than her, Janey realized, when she finally stood in front of him. Shorter, and not much older than Max.

"What are you two doing here?" he demanded. He waved the rifle barrel so close that she could smell the gunpowder. This was no time to be all manly. She swept the tuque from her head so her hair tumbled down to her shoulders. Maybe they'd get a little leeway if he thought she was "just a girl".

Caught off guard, the soldier stepped back to eye her up and down. His glance lingered over her jeans before he came close again, trying to get into Janey's face. The fact that he was shorter than her appeared to irritate him. "You're a little young to be rolling around in the hay with a whelp like this'un, aren't ya? Is he payin' or are ya givin' it away?"

In the instant before she raised her hand to smack him, the soldier flew backwards into the bushes. She looked at her hand, stunned, then realized what had happened. Max had punched a soldier. A soldier with a rifle. Before she could calculate the costs, Max pulled her into the forest. Another bullet flew past them and they froze.

"So help me I will empty this rifle into ya both," the soldier shouted at them. "And I'd have every right. Assaultin' an officer. Aidin' and abettin' the escape of an enemy alien. Immoral conduct."

"What enemy alien?" Janey shrieked, her heart beating wildly. "You have no right –"

"We'll see who has rights around here," the soldier said. "Hands up. Turn and face me." They did as they were told. "Now," the soldier continued. "Names."

"I'm Janey. Janey Kane. Who are you?"

"I'm askin' the questions around here," the soldier said. He turned to Max. "Name," he barked.

"Max Kane," Max said. Janey kept her face calm and still. "Cousins," Max said, tilting his head toward Janey.

"Kissin' cousins?" the soldier asked, sneering.

"Look," said Janey, "this is really uncomfortable. I want to put my hands down."

"You can want all you want," the soldier said, switching his attention to her. "But you're gonna keep 'em up and march back to camp."

"What camp? And why? And what's your name?" She wracked her brain for the dialogue of old army movies. "And rank? And serial number? I demand some answers."

"Well aren't you Miss High 'n' Mighty," the soldier said. "You can demand all ya want, missy. But ya can't go around sluggin' those of us willin' to fight in this Great War." His voice dropped to a mutter. "Even if we gotta do it guardin' the same stinkin' Huns 'n' garlic eaters that killed my brother in some godforsaken trench overseas last year." He prodded Max in the back. "I'm not even gonna ask why this one ain't in uniform. Walk. Straight ahead until I say so. You get behind him." He nodded at Janey.

She started walking, aware that the soldier was only a

rifle-length behind her. But at least she had some answers. The soldier had called this the Great War. That's what they called the First World War before the second one erupted. It meant she and Max had travelled to somewhere after 1914. And a camp with "Huns and garlic eaters"? They were stumbling toward one of those internment camps they'd read about at the museum this morning. Which meant that the first man they saw, the skinny one with the beard, must have been an escaping prisoner.

"We didn't have anything to do with that guy running away," she said, turning to look at her captor. That's when her foot caught a root and she tripped. Max helped her up.

"Can we at least walk with our hands down?" Janey asked. "I can't keep my balance."

The soldier grunted but let them walk normally. When they reached a footpath, Janey and Max had enough room to walk side by side. Occasionally the back of his hand touched the back of hers. It was oddly comforting, she thought, given the rifle poking at their backs. She was still puzzling over why Max had used her last name and said that they were cousins, when they reached a double row of barbed wire. She and Max stopped, unsure.

"Follow the fence around to your left," the soldier ordered. Beyond it, a series of large canvas tents huddled together, partially hidden by a line of what had to be outhouses, their stink clearly identifying their purpose.

"Where is everyone?" Janey asked.

"Workin'," the soldier said. "Well, except for the two in the hoosegow. And the ones in the kitchen."

"What's a hoosegow?" Janey asked.

"You know. The hoosegow, the pokey, the stockade. The

jail. It's where you're gonna end up, the two of ya, if ya don't watch out."

"There's a jail inside the jail?"

"This ain't a jail, it's an internment camp."

"What's the difference?"

"Enough with your questions! Through this gate. Now."

The opening led them past the barbed wire and into a muddy meadow that looked as if it had been churned by hundreds of feet trudging the same way day after day. They approached a tent, smaller than most, but as grey and mouldy as all the rest. A stove pipe poked through the top and wisps of smoke drifted reluctantly from it.

"Captain Vernon! Captain Vernon sir!" the soldier called out.

A tent flap flipped open to reveal a man in a white shirt, suspenders and the same brownish-yellow pants as those of the soldier.

"Private Donaldson?"

"Yes sir! A prisoner escaped this morning, sir. But I found these two lurkin' in the same place, sir."

"And you thought you'd do a two-for-one exchange?" The captain looked at the three figures in front of him skeptically.

"And that one assaulted me, sir." Janey turned to see the soldier, Donaldson, pointing at Max.

"That was me," Janey jumped in. She didn't want either of them to end up in the horsegow or the hoosegow or whatever it was called, but it would probably go easier on her as a girl. "He said some rude things to me and I...I hit him."

"Their names are Max and Janey Kane, sir. They claim to be cousins," Donaldson added.

"If the private here was saying rude things, Mr. Kane – not that I even know what he said – but if he was, why were you not the one to defend your cousin's honour?" the captain asked.

"I don't need anyone else to fight my fights," Janey jumped in. "I don't need a man…or, or a boy…cousin…to do it for me. I can stand up for myself." She glared fiercely at them all, even Max.

The captain's mouth twitched. "Where are you two from? And why are you out here?"

"We're visiting in Banff because of my cousin's health," Janey said, hoping that would explain why Max wasn't in uniform. She'd been thinking of a cover story as they walked to the camp. "We were on a tour to see animal tracks when we were separated from our party and we got lost and suddenly bullets were flying and we had to dive for cover and then he found us," Janey explained. "All we want to do now is get back to Banff."

"But I found 'em right where Prisoner 314 ran off," Donaldson said. "I think there's something suspicious goin' on here, Captain."

You have no idea, Janey thought. She looked at the captain. "Can you point us in the right direction back to the Banff Springs Hotel, where our families are probably worrying about us?"

"Captain –"

"That's enough, Private Donaldson," said the captain, before turning to Janey. "The Banff Springs, did you say? I'm surprised the hotel is open this early in the season, but I suppose with the war on, everything changes." He considered.

"Private Donaldson, take them to the mess for now.

When the prisoners come back I'll assign one of the guards to find horses and escort these two back to Banff."

"But –"

"Private, I believe you let a prisoner escape this morning. I realize your infirmity may have hindered your pursuit." The captain glanced meaningfully at Donaldson's feet. "However, you have been accused of saying something disrespectful to a young lady. No. No interruptions. You have little else to add to this discussion. You are dismissed." He stepped back into his tent and pulled the flap back down.

"Well if that doesn't beat all," Donaldson grumbled. He turned to face them. Only then did Janey notice that Donaldson was limping.

"What's wrong with your foot?" she asked.

"None of your business," he said, scowling. "I can still be a good soldier an' fight for King an' country even with one leg shorter than the other. They'll send me over one o' these days." He prodded Max with the rifle to get him moving.

Janey put her hand on the barrel. "Just point us to where we should go. You don't even have to come with us."

"Don't you feel sorry for me," Donaldson spat out. "I can still do my duty. You really must be a big-time mucky-muck, a girl like you, wearing pants, speaking up the way ya do, asking questions an' ordering the likes of me around." His eyes narrowed. "What makes ya think you're better 'n' me?"

Janey had had enough. She squared her shoulders and pulled herself up to her full height, so that she was looking down at Donaldson. "Let's clear some things up. The muck is on the grounds of this camp. We're all walking in it. But even more importantly," she said, speaking crisply so he'd be sure to understand, "I don't think I'm better than you. I think we're exactly equal. Even with you waving that rifle around. Now, where's the mess?"

The line of the private's mouth straightened into a tight grimace. Silently, he pointed toward a larger tent, further into the camp. "Let's go, Max," Janey said. Unfortunately, the mud made it difficult for her to stride away regally. Instead, they both squelched toward the dingy grey shelter.

Lifting a sodden flap, they stepped inside. Long rows of rough-hewn benches and tables lined the interior. Two pot-bellied stoves squatted in the middle of the tent, cold and black. At the far end, a second canvas wall dangled from the roof. Because it didn't quite reach the ground, it revealed the muddy boots of several people who sounded as if they were clanging pots and pans together with a vengeance. A faint smell of – cabbage? potatoes? – hung in the air. Janey suddenly realized that she was cold and famished. A hot drink would be just the thing. Maybe they'd have something on a stove back there.

Before she took a second step, Max tugged her back. She looked at him, annoyed.

"I'm trying to –" But Max put a finger to her lips.

He pulled her to a bench and sat down beside her. "We have to be careful here," he said in a low voice.

"What for? We're safe from that gun-toting idiot, and I'd kill for a cup of something hot," Janey said, getting up and putting her tuque back on for warmth. She pulled up the collar of her jacket. "They probably have some tea or something back there."

Max yanked her down again. "You don't understand. This is an internment camp. There are no chocolates on your pillow at night or room service or hot tea or coffee to take away.

There is nothing good here," he spat out. And then he began to shiver.

Janey looked at him. Max seemed smaller, somehow more terrified than when those bullets had whizzed past him. It was as if fear had shrunk him down and squished him into a tiny box. Time travelling, especially the first time, was confusing and disorienting, but something more was going on with Max.

"Why did you say we were cousins?" she asked suddenly.

"Because you have a good English name," he said bitterly. "Because you speak without any accent at all."

"So? What does that have to do with anything?"

Max looked away, miserable. "Because here, now, I am the enemy. I am an enemy alien."

Janey could have smacked herself. Of course! That's why he'd said hardly anything. Thanks to his Canadian mother his English was pretty good, but who knew what could cause a slip-up. She put her hand on his shoulder, hoping to still his shivering, but he shrugged it away.

"I wish I'd never followed you through that door. I wish I'd never come here to Banff. I wish...I wish..." His voice faded away.

How odd, thought Janey, to have her own thoughts from the last two days coming out of Max's mouth. But it must all be worse for him, with his accent and his "enemy" background.

"We'll get out of here, Max, I promise. Everything'll be all right," she said, kneeling next to him. "Besides, you owe me a waltz at that stupid staff Christmas party."

Max snorted, anger flashing across his face. "Nothing is all right," he hissed. "Stop being so..."

His voice trailed off as the tent flap lifted and a group of men shambled into the mess, deep voices grumbling and calling out to one another. Janey recognized some German words in the flow of what had to be Ukrainian. But when one of the men caught sight of her, he switched to English.

"Hey, we got company," he said. Four figures ambled over, then about a half-dozen more. Lean and dirty, dressed in caps and thin coats, they crowded around Janey and Max. Everything was dull and grey, from their clothing and their skin to the streaks of mud on their flimsy boots. Janey felt as if she was looking at one of those old-fashioned sepia photos where objects could only be made out by the varying shades of black and white. They had to be the internees, one grimy, grizzled enemy alien barely distinguishable from the next.

The only patch of colour was a dirty red cotton kerchief around the neck of a man who looked, Janey realized, much younger than the rest. In fact, he could have been about Max's age. He stood quietly at the back, bright blue eyes peering from a dirt-smudged face, next to an older man with a rasping cough.

Another internee pushed to the front. "Are you new guards? Uniforms good," he said in broken English. Someone muttered something Janey couldn't understand and they all laughed. More comments, fetid and sour-sounding, wafted from the men as they crowded around, hemming her in. A grimy hand, only partially covered with an old, worn sock, reached out to touch her. Max's hand shot out and caught the dirty one by the wrist. Max said something in a low, urgent voice, and again, Janey couldn't understand.

But the response was electric. The muttering ceased and

the prisoners stared at them, mouths open. Slowly they turned to look at each other. Finally, the boy with the red kerchief made his way forward and said something to Max. Max nodded.

Janey turned to him. "What? What's he saying? And what are you saying?"

But Max was busy asking more questions. The boy responded, then held out his hand. "Stefan," he said.

Max shook it, said his own name, and pointed to Janey. "Fraulein Kane," he said.

Now it was Janey's turn to lift her jaw from the floor. "Why are you speaking to him in German? Aren't you the one who was worried about...you know..." She gestured with her head toward the prisoners.

"We will be still," Stefan said eagerly. He said something to the other prisoners and they all nodded. "My father –" He pointed to the frail man with the cough who stood beside him, "and all these men –" He indicated the others in the group. "We will not speak about this." They all nodded again, but then they all began to talk at once.

Max stood and held up his hands, motioning for quiet. He asked questions and Stefan responded, eager to answer. Janey could only watch as anger, sadness and more anger flitted across the men's creased, drawn faces.

Other men shuffled in from outside, where the day was fading into twilight. Someone lit the stoves and the new crowd moved toward them, keener to warm themselves than to see what was going on. Still Janey fretted. What if word got out that Max was Austrian, or at least, that he could speak German? What if they couldn't get out of the camp? What if they couldn't get back to their normal lives?

And the biggest question of all wasn't a *what if*, but a *why*. Why on earth was Janey here in a First World War internment camp?

The questions disappeared when Janey saw the mess flap lift briskly and Donaldson come in. "Soldier Crooked Leg comes," one of the internees said. Some of the others grinned. Janey almost felt sorry for the private.

"Beautiful mountains, miss," Stefan said in English. He nodded at Janey's neckline. "I like very much." Janey's fingers rose to what had caught his eye and she found the pin she'd attached to the collar of her sweater that morning.

"Thank you," she said gravely, as Donaldson barrelled through the crowd.

"Move along, ya lazy foreigners," he said, shoving the prisoners roughly aside. "Did I hear you fraternizing with the enemy, Miss Kane?" Janey lost her sympathy for the soldier.

"We just to practise our English with the miss," Stefan said. The other prisoners nodded in agreement.

Donaldson turned on Stefan. "Did I ask ya anything, ya worthless piece of murdering foreign turd? Step back from here. Step back from this table. All of ya or ya'll all be on half rations. Do I make myself clear?"

The crowd moved back, grumbling, but the private's stare forced them into silence. "Now then," he said, turning back to Janey and Max, the contempt in his face not softening. "I have the high honour of escorting you two back into Banff. On foot. 'Cuz we can only spare two horses. Ain't that a treat? Follow me."

He led them out of the mess, letting the tent flap snap back into Max's face. Before she slipped through, Janey waved to Stefan, a small, thoughtful figure in the crowd of grubby, defeated men.

Donaldson limped ahead of them to a corral and the only two horses it contained. "The two of ya can ride, can't ya?" he asked, smirking as he handed the reins of a small, down-in-the-mouth buckskin mare to Janey, and a steel grey stallion with frightened eyes to Max.

Since she'd moved out west, Janey had taken enough trail rides with Nicky and Michael to pick up some tips about riding. She checked the cinch to make sure it was done up right, stuck her foot in the stirrup and hoisted herself up.

"Glad to see I didn't need to rustle ya up a side-saddle," Donaldson said, sneering.

"Good thing I'm wearing these practical clothes, then," Janey said, nudging the mare with her heels. It didn't budge. She tried again, squeezing her legs against the horse's flanks. Still nothing.

Meanwhile, Max's horse wouldn't stop moving. Max tried several times to approach the side of the stallion, but it kept skittering away. He put a hand on its neck and started to say something, then caught himself. He'd been about to speak to it in German, Janey realized. Instead, Max shushed the animal gently in English and tried again. It sidestepped the mount.

"What's wrong with it?" Janey asked Donaldson.

"It's shy," the private said, smirking as he watched Max and the horse dance around each other.

"Can't we get another one?" Janey asked.

Donaldson snorted and startled the stallion just as Max was settling it. "Another one? Are ya kiddin' me? Look around! Other than a few wild ones like this stallion, there are barely any horses left here. They've all gone overseas to fight and die, shot and killed or gassed to death by the same animals we have here."

It took Janey a few moments to pick apart Donaldson's blending of horses, animals, soldiers and prisoners. She was about to ask him about his brother, but Max's movements caught her eye. He'd crowded the stallion against the corral's fence so it couldn't move away. Holding the reins in one hand, he rocked the saddle horn from side to side with the other, forcing the horse to balance itself by spreading its legs. In one quick motion Max stepped into a stirrup and mounted. The horse bolted forward but Max brought it to a stop outside the camp gates. Not bad, thought Janey, trying once more to get her own horse to move.

Donaldson grabbed her reins and yanked her horse toward Max. "Looks like your cousin knows a thing or two about horsemanship," he said as they moved down the path through a thick stand of fir trees, out of sight of the camp. Max and the stallion waited for them a short distance ahead. "And that's why I think two of ya can ride the grey horse an' I'll mosey along on the mare."

"Wait a minute," Janey said, panic rising. "You want me to ride that thing? No way."

Donaldson brought her horse to a stop. Try as Janey might, she couldn't urge the little brown mare forward.

"Look," Donaldson said. "I ain't walking all the way into town. Just 'cuz I said somethin' to someone who's supposed to be my betters don't mean that's a fair punishment. An' I ain't ridin' that stallion. We don't like each other, but it'll follow this mare home. So since your *cousin* can handle that grey demon so well, you climb on with him. We'll all be on horses. And that way the rules for me and you and your cousin will be exactly equal." He looked up at her, daring her to defy what she'd said earlier.

Max circled his horse until it was next to Janey's. "C'mon," he said, holding out his hand to her, urging her with his eyes, because, in front of Donaldson, he didn't trust the accented words on his tongue.

Before she could reconsider, Janey pulled her outside foot over her saddle, placed it in the stallion's stirrup and swung her other leg behind Max. As soon as she settled her weight on the horse, it took off. Janey grabbed at Max, trying desperately to hang on. Donaldson's shouts and angry commands disappeared under the galloping hooves of their horse. Janey could only hope the shouts wouldn't be followed by bullets.

"Slow down," she called, but Max was busy dipping under tree branches and holding on himself. She could only follow the movements of his body, tilting when he did, ducking when he did, her arms clinging fiercely to him as the forest flew by.

And then Max's shout: "*Verdammt!*"– full of fear and bravado, just as she sensed the horse gathering its strength to leap into the air. Over something? Down something? Janey couldn't see what Max saw. But she felt him kick loose his stirrups and then the two of them were flying sideways off the horse. All Janey could do was close her eyes tight and hold on.

CHAPTER FIVE

Something small and jagged bounced down the side of Janey's head, rolling to a stop by her nose. She opened her eyes. A pine cone, its brown scales jammed with snow, sat wedged between her face and Max's back. Was he hurt? Was she? Janey tried to sit up, but her left arm was trapped under him and he wasn't moving. She stared at his back. A small, steady rise and fall reassured her that, at the very least, he was breathing.

How long had they been lying here? And where was Donaldson? It was a wonder he wasn't standing over them, jabbing them with his rifle. And their horse? No sign or sound of him either.

Great. No horse. No food. Not even a sense of the direction they should be going. She closed her eyes, trying to block out the mess that she'd landed in, but her thoughts kept swirling.

What was the point of meeting a Nakoda family one time, and then a bunch of First World War internees the next? And why was this kid from Austria lying here next to her, slowly crushing her arm as pine cones stuffed with snow rained down on her and –

Wait. Snow?

Janey raised her head to look around properly. Yup, snow. Mountains of it, in snow banks, on tree branches, against – yes! – their hotel! They were back in the present! Excitedly, she whacked Max with her free hand.

"Max! Get up! We're back!" She was almost giddy with relief. If only she could get up.

He groaned and rolled over. They were almost nose to nose. The thought flitted through Janey's mind that it wasn't a bad nose. When Max wasn't scowling or looking worried, it wasn't even a bad face. And he'd been kind of awesome just now, slugging ol' Donaldson, keeping his cool in the camp, handling that horse –

Max's eyelids fluttered open. He had the bluest eyes, she thought, feeling his breath on her cheeks. Wait, this was weird. She pulled back, trying to yank her arm out from under him. A branch she'd been lying on released and popped into another snow-laden one above, showering white stuff all over them. They scrambled up and away from the tree.

"Well, at least we're not hurt," Janey said, brushing snow out of her hair.

Max's gaze swept from the hotel to the long-limbed tree and the imprints of their bodies in the knee-deep snow. "What's going on? How did we get here?"

"Well, you followed me out and we heard a gunshot and a soldier took us to a camp and then we rode a horse..." Janey's voice trailed off. Max was staring at her as if she was speaking Latin. Or Greek. Or some other language that *he* didn't understand. For once.

Or maybe he did understand her, but he really hadn't been at that internment camp. What if she'd imagined that Max had time-travelled with her? Maybe they'd simply left the hotel, come out here and somehow fallen into the bottom boughs of this evergreen tree.

No. The time travel had to be real. Max was just not ready to –

"This is crazy," Max said, backing away from her. "There's no horse here, no guns, no gunshot. Stay away from me. I don't need this in my life right now." He spun around and hurried to the hotel.

She kicked furiously at the snow at her feet, wishing it was less fluffy and had more pack so she could scoop it into snowballs to whip into his stiff, retreating back.

Her final kick sent something bouncing along the concrete into more snow on the other side of the path. She stooped and brushed away some of the white stuff and discovered Max's pin. It looked as if the tiny, silver mountains were buried in an avalanche.

She plucked it out and studied that single word, *Remember*, more closely. Remember what? All she wanted to do was forget. She dropped it into her coat pocket and trudged back to the hotel.

"Lovers' quarrel?"

Janey looked up. Sam the bellman was holding a door open for her.

"It wasn't a...we're not...we just met yesterday," Janey spat out.

"Sorry, sorry," Sam said, hands up, as if in surrender. "I saw you guys dancing last night and then you..." His voice trailed off as Janey's glare dropped the temperature around them to sub-zero.

She steamed past him into the lobby and nearly ran over a little girl in a frilly dress who was standing, nonplussed, in the middle of her path. "I had brunch with Santa," she said, eyes wide.

Janey couldn't help smiling. "Was it fun?"

The little girl nodded, even as her dad led her back to where the family was sitting.

Janey took in the chattering children, the twinkling

lights and the holiday decorations, and let them lift her spirits. So what if she and Max didn't become BFFs? So what if he didn't want to think about what had happened? Really, maybe she shouldn't think about it either. Maybe all this time travelling was just a part of the Christmas magic. Instead of worrying about it, she should simply enjoy her stay here at the hotel until they could go home and put up the Christmas tree and be with her family. She winked at the little girl, who was now on her dad's lap, and made her way to the elevator.

It was hard to hang on to that cheerfulness when she opened the door to the suite.

"Oh, Janey. You missed your dad's phone call." Granny closed the stopper on a bottle of nail polish and looked up, worried.

"He called? Here? What did he want? Is everything all right?" For the millionth time, she wished she hadn't lost her cell phone.

"Everyone's fine, just fine. He wanted to see how we were doing," Granny said, waving her hands in the air to let her nails dry. "And to tell us that he's lost his passport. Well, he didn't lose it. Someone stole it."

"No! How?" Janey dropped onto the couch.

"They were in a market crowded with people, and by the time Alex figured out that the person mashed against him had his fingers in his pocket, the thief was gone."

"That's awful. Is he okay?"

"Really, he's fine. But…there's a problem."

Janey frowned. "He can get another passport, can't he?"

"Yes, but since it's just before Christmas, everything slows down and he might not get a new one until January."

"No!" Janey sprang up from the couch. "He won't be here? No! How could he be so...so stupid and careless? Didn't he think? It's as if he's planned it. First he leaves here just before Christmas and now he's worked out a way so we can't all be together." She stopped her pacing. "What about Mum? Will she be able to come back?"

The door to Charlie and Max's bedroom swung open and Max stepped out, glowering at Janey. "My grandfather is trying to make a phone call overseas," he said icily. "Could you please speak more quietly?"

Janey stared at him, almost at a loss for words. Her dream of a cozy holiday with her family had disappeared with the flick of a pickpocket's wrist, and he wanted her to calm down? She could only take so much of this.

"Listen, jerk!" Janey said, going around the coffee table and right up into his face. "You can go ahead and be all snotty and bossy but right now go do it somewhere else, okay? I really don't want to deal with you. You think I want to be here? I'd way rather be at home spending Christmas with my own family..."

"Now, Janey!" Granny was getting to her feet.

"Well at least you have a family!" Max shouted back at her.

"Yeah, I know your mother died. That's awful. But it happened years ago, and you need to deal with it and stop being so moody and –"

Charlie's voice cut in. "I'm sorry, Max. Still no news about your dad's whereabouts. But they may have a lead on the kidnappers."

Janey swung around. Charlie was standing in the doorway of the bedroom, a rumpled Santa with tired eyes full of disappointment.

Confused, Janey turned from Charlie to Granny, then finally to Max. "Kidnappers?"

Charlie was looking at his grandson. "Max, I don't think we should keep secrets anymore. Also, I told Amanda weeks ago."

"Told her what?" Janey looked from one person to the next.

"But –" Max began.

"Son, you need friends right now. Tell her. I think Janey will keep your secret and not ruin any police negotiations."

Max looked out the window for a moment, and Janey realized he was collecting himself. When he turned back to her, his eyes were pale and frightened.

"My father was kidnapped 39 days ago. Near Hungary. Or in Hungary. We don't know. Or the police don't know." Max's voice was low and miserable.

Janey had to sit down. It occurred to her that they'd both been counting days until they saw a parent again, but his reasons were way, way more serious. "Why? Why was he kidnapped?"

Max shrugged. "Because he works to stop human trafficking. And the traffickers don't want it to stop. So they try to stop him."

"That's so horrible." Janey shook her head. "But aren't they just helping people who want to get away from a war or a famine in their own country?"

"No. Those are human smugglers. There's a difference," said Max. "The smugglers are bad enough. They put people on leaky boats or in containers with no air and bring them across borders. That's also criminal. But human traffickers take poor people, even children younger than us, and bring them across borders to sell like slaves. The people who are trafficked don't want to be taken away."

This was what he'd been talking about at the museum, Janey realized. "And your dad was trying to stop this?"

Max nodded. "He works for an organization that tries to stop this kind of crime. But it's hard. The traffickers are rich and powerful. They're evil, horrible people. They stole my father just like they stole all the other people." He looked away. Charlie put an arm around his shoulder and led him to the opposite couch.

Janey's thoughts reeled. Human trafficking? Kidnapping? Was this even for real? She turned to her grandmother for confirmation, but her attention was on Max, who had buried his head in his hands.

"Max, son. It'll be okay. It will," Charlie said firmly, sitting down next to his grandson and patting his knee. "Wasn't that phone call yesterday evening good news?"

"That was almost 24 hours ago," Max said glumly. "We haven't heard anything since."

That was the call when everybody froze, Janey remembered, and then Max and Charlie both rushed to get it. "What was it about?" she asked.

"One of the detectives on my father's case. She'd heard of a man who got away from a factory near the border." Janey watched the muscles on Max's jaw clench and release.

"When we talked to her just now, she'd found the man and got names and possible addresses of the kidnappers. But they still don't know where my dad is. Or if he's still…"

Janey would bet a ticket to Cambodia that the word *alive* was now dancing in all four of their heads, like some sour, bitter sugarplum. She looked away. Wow. While she was worrying about getting a Christmas tree up in time, this guy was wondering if his only remaining parent was okay. Or even still breathing.

"Well, we can hope, can't we," Granny said briskly. She patted Max on the back and moved toward the little kitchen. "I'm making hot chocolate. Does anyone else want some?"

"I'm so sorry, Max. This just sucks for you," Janey said, flopping down beside him. He nodded and rubbed a sleeve over his face. She'd been reading him wrong this whole time. He wasn't being smug or superior; he was trying to hold it all together. She'd thought it was all about her, when he really had so much more to worry about. And the constant phone checks? It all made sense now. She touched his hand. "Really, I'm sorry."

"Thanks," he said, looking up only briefly before wiping his sleeve across his face again.

Charlie had disappeared into his bedroom and returned waving a brochure. "We could all use a break," he said. The brochure caught a branch of the tree, knocking it over. As the red balls flew across the carpet, Janey couldn't help herself. The look of horror on Charlie's face made her giggle.

"I'd say that tree needs a break," said Granny from the kitchen. "Unless you killed...it." Horrified at having used the word *killed*, Granny clapped her hand over her mouth, and Janey stopped giggling.

"I think it's trying to kill *us*," Charlie said seriously. "It keeps throwing itself at our feet so we'll trip over it." Janey couldn't help it. She started giggling again. Granny snorted.

"The killer Christmas tree," Max intoned as he eyed it suspiciously. Laughter erupted from the other three, growing so loud and infectious that Max was soon chuckling with the rest of them. They hunted for the escaped tree decorations in all the corners of the room. Max even discovered two foil-wrapped chocolate balls under the furthest couch and grinned as Janey took one. By the time they'd set the tree to rights in a safer corner of the living room, everyone was in a better mood.

"What I was going to say, before I was so rudely interrupted, was that we should all go skiing tomorrow," Charlie announced. "I have nothing on until the ball tomorrow night and it would do us all a world of good to get away. I'll ask Sam to help me sneak out of the hotel."

"Skiing would be super," Max said. "What time can we start? 7:30? But I'll need to rent skis. 6:30?"

"Whoa," Charlie said, seeing the shocked look on Janey's face. "I think we can leave a little later than that. Let's aim for 8 o'clock." The expression on Janey's face hadn't changed. "Or 8:30, and we'll have the whole day to ski. Maybe Lake Louise tomorrow and Sunshine or Nakiska on Friday."

Only Granny looked less than excited.

"Don't you worry, Amanda. I'll take the kids skiing and you can spend the whole day at the spa, being pampered for the ball."

"Well that's a relief," Granny said. "I've never seen the appeal of thundering down the side of an icy mountain strapped to two tiny wisps of wood."

Unlike Granny, Janey loved skiing, but she was no expert. So the sight of the moguls tumbling down the steep hill under the chair lift had her feeling a little queasy. It didn't help that Max was making the chairlift sway.

"Stop," she said, and when he didn't, she punched him in the arm. He grinned at her, but the chairlift steadied. A winter sun streamed down, warm enough to make them take off their mitts to cool their sweaty hands. Charlie had met two former work colleagues and was riding up with them, so Janey and Max had the chair to themselves.

Max fiddled with a buckle on his boot, then sat up and sighed. "This is good," he said, and it took Janey a moment to realize he wasn't talking about the fit of his footwear. He twisted to look at the mountain behind them, taking in the pattern of the runs on Larch and the curl of smoke from Temple Lodge.

"As good as your Alps?" Janey asked teasingly.

Max considered her question seriously. "Different, I think. These Rockies are much more...wild. People have lived in our Alps for many, many centuries."

"People have lived here for just as long," Janey said, remembering Mary and her family. "But the First Nations didn't build castles or churches to leave their mark. They moved around, depending on where the food was."

Max nodded. "Yes. When you have mountains like these, you don't need cathedrals to scratch at the sky."

"Those are nice too, though," she said. She touched his hand. Startled, Max looked first at his hand and then at her.

"I...I want to say again that I'm sorry," Janey rushed on. "I'm sorry about what I said about your mum. And this horrible thing with your dad. I didn't know."

Max studied her. "Thanks." A grin snuck across his face. "You do have an interesting temper." Before Janey could respond, he held up his hands. "But yesterday, at the museum,

I was a jerk. I'm sorry too."

Janey ignored the comment about her temper. "That's okay. Now I get why you were so upset. But the detective's phone calls last night and the night before are good news, right?"

"Yes. It was the first good news we've had in many weeks. I hope…I hope they find him soon."

"It'll happen," Janey said. They settled back into a friendly silence. This *was* good, she thought. Max was actually okay. But he hadn't mentioned anything about being at the internment camp yesterday. Still, given everything that was going on in his life, it made sense that he didn't want to believe he'd time-travelled with her. Too much crazy right now. Yet the more she thought about it, the more she believed they had gone back together. It was just a matter of figuring out why.

"What do you think…" she began, but they'd reached the end of the lift and he was getting ready to jump off.

"Race you," he challenged.

She slid off the lift after him and they skied toward the top of the run where they'd agreed to wait for Charlie.

"Max," she tried again. "What do you think about yesterday? About the internment camp?"

He glanced at her, his smile disappearing. "I said I was sorry. But I still think it was awful."

"No, I mean about being there," Janey said. "About meeting Stefan and…the others."

"I don't know what you're talking about," Max said. And then he was gone, skimming effortlessly down through the moguls, away from her and from any discussion of yesterday's events.

Snow sprayed across her skis as Charlie pulled up beside

her. "Show off," Janey muttered.

He grinned. "I don't think I'll hold out until 1 o'clock for lunch. I have to keep up my fine Christmas physique. How about we meet at Temple Lodge, upstairs, at 12:30?"

"Sure," Janey said. "You'll have to catch up with Max and tell him, because I'm sticking to the blue runs."

"Easy," said Charlie. He plunged down the hill after his grandson. She could see where Max got his style, at least when it came to skiing.

Janey veered left, choosing a longer, gentler run that would let her concentrate less on skiing and more on what had happened since she and Granny had shown up at the hotel. She could do nothing about her dad's lost passport and the mess it would create for Christmas. She turned instead to the time travelling. Was yesterday's escapade some sort of glitch in the system? Maybe Max wasn't supposed to come along, and that's why he didn't remember anything. Because after all, the first time she'd gone back it was in 1883, when those railroad guys stumbled into the cave. The internment camp didn't happen until the First World War started in 1914. So what was the connection? And even if she'd taken a detour into the wrong period with Max, why was she going back in the first place? What was she supposed to fix? Granny couldn't remember any historical family ties to Banff. Was her mother's side of the family the reason? Janey'd have to ask the next time they could talk.

Or maybe this had nothing to do with anything and Max was right and she was…just a little bit crazy. Because nobody really time-travels. All the bumps and bruises on the side of her leg could have come from slipping on an icy sidewalk and not from jumping down a vent hole or being thrown from a horse. Did Max even know how to ride? She should ask him at lunch. But the bite mark on her should –

"Hey Jo!"

Janey's slow, even slalom nearly dissolved into a tangle of skis and poles. Only one person ever called her that. She searched the hillside and there, just below her, stood Michael.

All of the complicated feelings that she'd carefully packed away when Michael left last fall stirred, ever so slightly, somewhere deep inside her. What was going on?

She skied down and pulled up beside him. "Hey."

"Hey yourself," he said. They stared at each other. The hoots and shrieks of skiers and snowboarders whipping past couldn't pierce the quiet that settled around them.

"Nice curves," Michael finally said, breaking the spell and grinning at her. "On the slopes, I mean." Then he body-checked her into the snow, lost his own balance and crashed down on top of her.

"Get off me, you big goof." Janey's laughter turned to shrieks when Michael took a handful of snow and started scrubbing her face with it.

"Who's the goof now?" he asked, then gasped as the snow Janey was stuffing down the front of his jacket hit bare skin.

"All right, all right! Truce," he called, rolling away. They lay there for a moment, picking snow and ice crystals from bits of their clothing.

"So, what are you doing here?" Janey finally asked.

"Even hockey school has Christmas holidays," Michael said, getting to his feet. "Adam, a guy from my school, is from St. Albert and he and his dad offered to drive me home, with a detour to Banff first. I'm in Edmonton tomorrow night."

"The school must suit you," she said, rising. "You look

good." He'd grown even taller since she'd seen him last. She wondered if Maggie had seen him more recently.

"Yeah. I like it. But you're…looking good too."

Unsure of what else to say, Janey pushed off with her poles. "Race you to the lift!"

They flew down, swerving and laughing. Michael reached the lift line first and pivoted to face her as she pulled up. He was grinning broadly. "As a rule, I like to have a gorgeous brunette waiting for me at the chairlift. Preferably with a hot drink."

"So do I," she said, taking in the black curls peeking from under his helmet.

"I'm not a brunette," he said, indignantly.

"Or gorgeous," she said, poling by him toward the chairs.

Michael put out a hand to stop her. "Wait. I have to meet with my friends at the top of Larch. But I want to see you tonight. Where are you staying?"

"At the Banff Springs."

"Wow. Did you guys suddenly inherit a bunch of money?"

"Nope. It's through a friend of Granny's. It's great actually. But um…tonight I can't. There's this ball."

Michael's eyebrows rose. "A ball? As in a soccer ball?"

"No. You know. One of those things where you get dressed up and you dance and stuff."

"You? Dress up? I'd almost pay to see that," he said, smirking. "The girl I know loved being caked up to her eyelashes in mud."

Janey knew he was referring to a particularly wet and grimy soccer game last spring. She'd head-butted a ball and stopped a goal, but momentum sent her headfirst into a massive puddle, much to the amusement of the other players.

When she stood up, rivulets of muddy water flowing from her uniform into her cleats, she figured the only thing she could do was take a bow. So she did, to loud and enthusiastic cheering from the sidelines.

Balancing carefully on her skis, Janey repeated the bow. They couldn't stop grinning at each other.

"It's really good to see you again," Michael said.

"Yeah." They stood there, smiling at each other for what seemed like a minute.

Michael's expression grew more serious. "How come you never answered any of my texts?"

"I lost my phone. And I thought we'd agreed that –"

A blur of blue slashed to a stop beside them. "There you are. Grandfather says we should come in now. He says he can eat a cow." Max looked puzzled. "I think it was a cow."

"Michael, this is Max. He's the grandson of Granny's friend. We're all staying..." She paused. Michael didn't need to know they were all staying in the same suite. "...at the Banff Springs."

Max removed his glove and thrust out his hand. Michael shook it warily.

"It's *horse*, Max, not cow," Janey said quickly. Michael watched the two of them.

"Do you eat horses here? I thought only the French did that," Max said.

"No, we don't, usually, but the expression is –"

"Look, I've got to go," Michael said. "See you around, Jo." He was poling his way to the next chair before Janey could say anything else.

"Jo?" Max looked puzzled. "I thought your name was Janey."

"My real name is Johanna. Don't, don't say anything. I'm named after my grandmother on my mother's side. But my grandfather on my dad's side really, really wanted a granddaughter named Janey, so that's the name I mostly go by."

Max nodded. "My great-grandfather really, really wanted a girl named Grazia. So I have a great-aunt called Tante Grazia, and my father's sister is also Grazia. If I was born a girl, I think that would be my name too." He shuddered. "But Johanna is a good name. I like it."

"Let's stay with Janey," she said, watching Michael go up the lift, wishing she could have said something more to him. "And let's go in. I could eat a horse too." The lodge was behind them and slightly uphill, making her wish they'd stopped the race there.

"But why do you say 'I could eat a horse' when no one eats them here?"

"I don't know. It's one of those expressions." She reached the lodge and stepped out of her skis. "Speaking of horses, do you know how to ride them?"

His eyes narrowed briefly, but then he nodded, almost reluctantly. "My grandfather, he had a few horses where he lived in the country. He taught me to ride when I was little. And even to jump. But I haven't ridden since..." He paused, looking confused.

"Since yesterday?" Janey asked sweetly.

"I don't know what you are talking about," Max snapped, shoving open the lodge door. He clomped into the building, his heavy boots adding to the rumble of skiers thumping up the stairs and across the wooden floors of the timbered building.

They pushed by mounds of jackets hanging from posts

and piles of mitts and helmets balanced on benches and tables. They're gear moguls, Janey thought, weaving past them with care. She wondered if she should try to explain her new term to Max. Michael would have understood in an instant.

They found Charlie in a quiet nook upstairs, pulling a bottle of orange juice from the lunches they'd packed at the hotel.

"Ah, there you are. You kids having fun?"

"It's really super," Max said. "I found Janey at the lift. With a friend. A friend named Michael."

"Ah! How much of a friend is this friend named Michael?" Charlie asked. "And does Amanda know about him?"

He did make a perfect Santa, Janey thought, taking in the honest-to-goodness twinkle in his eye. "He's my best friend's brother, and yes, Granny knows him. They live down the street," she said. She took a big bite of her sandwich so she wouldn't have to answer anything else.

"Any phone calls?" Max asked.

Charlie shook his head. "I even checked for better reception down at the base. But we'll hear good news soon; I'm sure of it."

Janey swallowed her bite. "Max was telling me how he's been riding horses since he was little. He could probably ride anything, maybe even skittish grey stallions that aren't used to –"

"I'd like to try the expert runs on the other side of the mountain this afternoon. Will you show me, Grandfather?"

The frost that developed between Max and Janey at lunch

had grown into an icy wall between them on the ride back. So Janey didn't hesitate when the car paused at a red light and she saw her grandmother's tall, familiar figure stepping into a hair salon just off Banff's main street.

"I'm getting out here, Charlie. Granny's over there and I'll catch a ride back with her." She stepped out and shut the car door before Charlie could say anything. Max's face seemed to be glued to the window on the other side of the car.

A young woman was just taking Granny to her station when Janey walked into the busy salon.

"Hello kiddo," Granny said, smiling as she saw her granddaughter. "You here to keep me company? How was your day?" But before Janey could launch into details, Granny's smile disappeared. Janey turned to see the stylist at the next station give a long black braid to a young man just rising from her chair. He looked sad as, with one hand, he explored the back of his neck, a swath of stubbly short hair that matched the colour of the braid now in his other hand.

"Oh," said Granny. She approached the young man and asked him a quiet question. He nodded quickly and said something in reply. They exchanged a few more words before Granny gave his arm a squeeze. She stepped aside so he could pass to pay at the front of the salon.

Granny's stylist indicated that Janey could sit where the young man had been. On the other side of Granny's chair, another customer was having her hair wrapped in foils. As Granny's stylist swept a large cape around Granny's neck, the customer leaned over. "I'll bet he had that cut off because he has a court appearance," she said.

"Really?" Granny asked sharply. The customer shrugged. Granny's hands shot out from under her cape as she waved her stylist away and stood.

"Listen here," she said, swinging her neighbour's chair around so it faced her. "That boy just found out his grandmother died. Right before Christmas. As he was on his way home from university. He cut off his hair, the way many Cree people do, as a sign of mourning. Not because…" Granny paused and looked at the woman in disgust. "Ugh," she said and spun the chair so the woman faced the other way.

Granny glanced around the now-quiet salon. "You know what, Janey? I'll do my own hair. Let's go."

Granny emerged from the bathroom, her head encased in rollers, and tapped her granddaughter on the shoulder. "Help me with this zipper." Janey rose to fasten the red dress.

"What do you think?"

"It looks fabulous, Granny. You'll knock 'em dead. Or him. Though you should probably lose the rollers."

Granny gave Janey a quick hug. "Thanks for being so understanding about everything, from Charlie to my little fit at the salon."

"I thought you were pretty awesome," Janey said. "How did you know? About the braid, I mean."

"Remember, I was born in northern Alberta." The older woman looked at herself in the mirror and tugged sharply at her dress. "I just can't stand it when people automatically assume the worst." She shook her head. "Let's stop. Tonight is special. Go put your dress on. And I need to take these rollers out."

"You haven't heard anything about Dad and his passport,

have you?" Janey called to her grandmother's retreating back.

"Nope. Not a word."

Janey sighed. The scene in the salon had been a kind of relief, taking her mind away from her other problems. What if her parents didn't get to Canada in time? Last year, when her mum couldn't get home, had been bad enough. It had been just the three of them putting up all the familiar tree ornaments, without her mum to tell the stories that went with each one. This year, if it was just two of them, Christmas would be so...not Christmassy.

And there was tonight. Her brief détente with Max from this morning had dissolved in the ski chalet at lunch. She probably shouldn't have brought up the grey stallion. He'd barely said a word to her since then, though Charlie and Granny hadn't noticed anything. Why couldn't the Olds go to this ball on their own? Janey could stay here and catch up on some reading.

She even thought about calling Nicky, but what would they talk about? Not about Max, because the kidnapping was still a secret. And Janey had never talked to Nicky about Michael, because, well, for one thing, she was his sister, which made it weird, and for another, there really wasn't anything to tell. And the time-travel stuff? That was completely off limits.

So instead, she was going to a ball. She felt like a reluctant Cinderella as she slipped on the green dress, adjusting the short sleeves so it covered the bite mark on her shoulder.

At least *this* Cinderella didn't have to put on glass slippers, she thought, sliding her feet into new, low-heeled pumps that she'd tested by doing a couple of laps around the shoe store past a puzzled clerk. Janey hadn't cared. Unlike her grandmother, she prized shoes that she could run in. It meant she was ready for anything. Even waltzing.

She brushed her hair fiercely, caught it in a loose ponytail and pinned it to the top of her head, commanding it to stay. The garish orange pro wrap she used to keep her hair in place during soccer games was way easier to use than these clips and pins, but it clashed with the dress. She dug out her one tube of lip gloss and rubbed some on. So much for her makeup.

"Did you bring your silver locket? It would look great with your dress," Granny said, emerging from their bathroom in a cloud of hairspray.

"Honestly, Granny, you've probably shellacked all of our towels in there with that spray. And no, I think I left all my jewellery at home."

Granny stopped next to Janey, who was studying herself in the full-length mirror. "Head up; shoulders back," Granny murmured. They stood side by side, tall and determined, taking each other in.

"Two gorgeous gals," she said finally, and winked at Janey's reflection. "That dress really does bring out the colour of your eyes." She hugged her granddaughter to her. "I'm so lucky to have you around."

"Yeah, yeah. The things I do for you."

"Oh c'mon, it's not so terrible. Look, here we are in a castle, about to go to a ball. Pretty good for a girl like me from an outpost way up north."

She kissed her granddaughter lightly, then reached for a small, beaded purse, checking what was inside. "You know, it used to be I'd make sure I had a dollar and a dime in my purse when I went out. The dime was for a call at a pay phone if my date was a dud and the dollar was for the cab ride home. I guess I won't be needing those tonight."

Janey smiled. "I think you can still find a few phone booths here at the hotel, but the ride back up on the elevator will be free. You're not thinking your date's going to be a dud, are you?"

"Nah. I'm rambling." Granny watched as Janey scrambled through her backpack, trying to find a match for a lone, long-forgotten earring she'd discovered in one of her pockets. "How did I end up with a granddaughter who cared so little about jewellery and nice dresses?" she asked in mock dismay. "Stick on that Banff pin and we'll be ready to go."

The knock on their bedroom door came as Janey fastened the pin to the shoulder of her dress. Granny swept open the door and burst into laughter. Charlie stood there in full Santa regalia, holding out a white-gloved hand.

"The Polar Express awaits, my dear," he said. "Actually, it's the service elevator. You look stunning, by the way." Charlie winked at Granny before leading them out of the suite.

Sam hovered by the elevator, keeping the door open for them. "Step right in, the reindeer are restless," he said. Max was waiting inside, his crisp, light blue shirt picking up the flecks of blue in his dark suit. It made him look older, Janey thought, but still as serious.

"You look nice," she said, stepping in beside him. He glanced at her briefly, nodded, but said nothing. She sighed as the others stepped in and the doors closed. This was going to be a long night.

When the elevator opened again, Sam led them through a passageway into a ballroom of soft blues and golds. The crystal chandeliers twinkled, while masses of tea lights reflected off the gold decorations on each elegantly set table.

People clapped and cheered as Charlie walked in with Granny on his arm.

"Now isn't this wonderful," Granny said, as Sam pulled out her chair at a table marked *Santa*.

"The buffet opens at 8:30. By then most of the staff will be off work," Sam said. "But the bar is open, complete with all kinds of interesting juices." This was an aside to Janey and Max. "Please help yourselves. I'll be floating around if you need me." He nodded and headed to a table across the dance floor, crowded with co-workers all dressed up and ready to party. A stunning girl in a blue cocktail dress caught Sam's hand and pulled him into an empty seat beside her.

Charlie came over to Granny's side. "My dear, before you get yourself settled, would you mind doing the rounds with me?" he asked.

"Of course," Granny said. She rose and, taking Charlie's arm, left Janey and Max on their own. An awkward, gloomy silence lumbered onto the table between them.

This can't last, Janey thought, rising so quickly that she knocked her chair back. "I'm going to get –"

"I want some –"

"Juice," they both said. Janey grinned. "Look, let's make the Olds happy and get through this evening without fighting. After that, I promise I won't bother you anymore," she said, pulling her chair upright. She held out her hand. "Friends?"

Max only considered for an instant before shaking it. "Friends," he agreed.

"Good. Let's go check out the bar." She fell in beside him. "I guess you still haven't heard anything about your dad."

He shook his head. "No, nothing." They each chose

flutes of sparkling pomegranate juice and brought them back to the table.

"Here, let's toast to good outcomes," Janey said, holding up her glass.

"You can't toast with only juice," Max said, frowning. "There has to be –"

"No fighting, remember," Janey said.

Sheepishly, he clanked her glass and took a long drink. "It's this waiting. It's so hard," he said. "I thought if I came here to my grandfather, it would be easier than sitting in our empty apartment, having Tante Grazia calling every three hours. I felt like I was going a bit crazy. But there's nothing I can do. Except imagine what it must be like for him. Or if he's even still okay."

Janey took in his dejected air. "Don't give up. You have no reason to believe that he's not okay."

Max looked away. "Thank you." He glanced back. "Tell me about Michael. Are you good friends, if he can call you Jo?"

"Yeah, we're all friends from the neighbourhood. Me, him, his sister Nicky," Janey began, then stopped as Sam drifted up to the table.

"Hey, you two. You're being summoned." Sam tilted his head toward where Charlie and Granny stood on the dance floor, waiting for them.

"Now?" Max and Janey asked in unison.

"The dancing won't start till he leads off. And he says he won't lead off unless you guys are up there too."

Well, here goes nothing, Janey thought. *Head up; shoulders back.* She set down her glass and followed Max to where their respective grandparents were standing, a traditional Santa with a less traditional and more willowy Mrs. Claus at his side.

"Glad you two could join us," Max said cheerfully. "Are we all ready?"

A wave of panic washed over Janey. "I don't...I mean, I've never..."

"Relax," Max whispered. "You were good yesterday. Just remember to let me lead." As the strains of "The Blue Danube" waltz floated through the ballroom, he took her hand, and, placing his other hand in the small of her back, he pulled her toward him. "Let the music inside," he urged softly, his eyes blue and calm. "Ready?"

She nodded. He swept her away, first in large, easy spirals to the right, then in smaller, tighter circles to the left. The ballroom was spinning, a blur of blue the same colour as Max's eyes, but always in a steady, lilting rhythm that made her forget about the kidnapping of Max's father and the loss of her dad's passport and even whether time travelling was real. Nothing else mattered except the joy of moving fluidly and gracefully around the room. When it ended, she was surprised to see the floor had filled with other dancers.

She looked at him, stunned. "You can really dance," she said.

"You sound so surprised," Max said, as a new song began to play. "Listen, I wanted to ask –"

"Can I cut in?"

Janey swung round. "Michael? What are you doing here?" He looked great, she thought. Hockey players of a certain calibre had to arrive at their games dressed in suits and ties. Michael's was a silvery grey that fit him well, she thought.

Michael shrugged. "Adam's dad dropped me off after supper. I thought I'd check out the ballroom."

"Janey? I want to ask you something."

"What?" She turned back to Max.

"Not here," he said, looking over her shoulder at Michael.

"This is a great song," Michael said.

"Go away," Max ordered. "I need to ask her –"

"Oh, get lost," Michael said, stepping in front of Janey. "Just because you do some stupid first dance with her doesn't mean she's yours for the rest of the night."

"Wait a second," Janey said. "I'm still here. And I'm not anyone's to –"

The guys ignored her. "You don't even belong here," Max said to Michael. "Leave. Now."

"Max! Stop it. Michael!" People were staring and giving them space.

"You've got it wrong, dickhead. I belong here. You're the one who shouldn't be here. Go back to wherever you came from."

Someone shoved someone else and suddenly Max and Michael were on the floor, arms and legs thrashing, fists flying. This can't be happening, Janey thought, as dancers around them paused or pulled back. This was so stupid. And embarrassing. What were they thinking? Even worse, what was everyone else thinking? She looked up to see Charlie, Sam and that girl in the blue dress running toward them as the music stopped.

No, no, no. How was she supposed to explain this? And with all these people around? She had to get out of here. Desperately, she turned and spotted an exit past the table where they'd been sitting. She barrelled through onlookers, out of the ballroom and down a staircase, trying to get as far away as possible. She picked a hallway, then a turn, then a door.

By the time Janey stopped to catch her breath, she was on a crowded, dusty street in the heat of a summer day.

She'd done it again, she realized, trying to calm down and get her bearings. But when a length of rope dropped around her shoulders and tightened, she panicked. And when a pair of muscular hands scooped her off her feet, she screamed.

CHAPTER SIX

The crowd around Janey roared with laughter. She felt herself being dropped unceremoniously onto something that shifted slightly, even as she tried to find her balance. She was on a horse, she realized, her long green dress making her sit sidesaddle, though Janey could sense no saddle beneath her. She tried sliding off, but an arm, wrapped in intricate beading that extended from a pale leather glove, held her firmly in place. The horse moved forward.

"Stop. Stop fighting," a low, gruff voice urged. "You're safe."

"You got yourself a real pretty one there, Two Feathers," someone called. "Just make sure she doesn't fall off!"

Janey stilled. Two Feathers? As in Mrs. Two Feathers? Mary's mother?

She turned to look at the person who'd grabbed her. A weathered pair of eyes, shielded by the rim of an elaborate, beautifully decorated headdress, gazed back at her. The man who owned them was studying Janey as much as she was staring at him.

"Do you know Mary?" she asked.

He nodded. "She's my sister," he said.

Was this Peter? Or Jonas? But he looked older than her dad, she thought, taking in the lines and hollows that defined this man's face.

"Jonas?"

"Yup." His eyes twinkled. "Glad to see you're dressed better for this meeting than the last one. You're Janey, right?"

She nodded and peered at this middle-aged man. He'd been a boy two days earlier. Jonas Two Feathers must be feeling just as stunned as her, but she could only read amusement in his expression. Why wasn't he surprised? She opened her mouth to ask, but he cut her off.

"Wave," he ordered, and Janey, already confused, wondered why they couldn't say hello in the normal way. She held up her hand at him, and he rolled his eyes.

"Not at me. The people on the street."

For the first time since she'd left the disaster at the hotel, Janey looked around. Carriages and spectator stands lined the road, which was jammed with people clapping and cheering as she rode by. They weren't exactly cheering her, she realized, peering up the avenue. She was part of a long parade of men, women and children, all wearing brilliantly decorated jackets, shawls and leggings. Some walked, but many rode gorgeously outfitted ponies and horses. With every step they took, feathers, fringes and ropes of beads swayed in the light of a bright summer day.

"What is this?" Janey asked.

"The Indian Days Parade," Jonas said gravely. "Wave." Still trying to get her bearings, Janey did as she was told, waving and nodding as the parade ambled along. They were on a broad avenue featuring rustic log buildings and a few sturdy brick ones. Some were hotels or cafes; others offered wilderness tours or hiking gear. It all looked so familiar, she thought. Finally, it came to her.

"Are we in Banff?" she asked Jonas. He nodded again. That's one question out of the way, she thought. Now if she could only figure out why she was here and how to get back, she'd be all set. She stared at all the white faces peering from wagons, sitting on bleachers or standing on both sides of the road. In contrast to the river of colour that paraded down the middle of the street, the men on the sidelines had on dull, dark suits, while the women wore the palest of cotton dresses and straw hats. From up here they looked boring, Janey thought, even as they darted into the road to give coins to the smallest Indigenous children.

The procession slowed as it crossed the bridge over the Bow River. Some of the bystanders turned their attention to Janey and pointed at her.

"Should I even be up here?" she asked.

"*You* never know where you should be," Jonas said. "But Mary will want to see you."

"Mary? Is she –"

"Well, if it ain't the famous Miss Kane," called a belligerent voice from the edge of the road. "Switched out your so-called cousin for an Indian, did ya?"

Janey stiffened and scanned the crowd. At the back stood a young man in the same ugly brownish-yellow army issue jacket and pants as...Private Donaldson. Oh no. Him? She'd barely given the soldier a thought since she'd left the internment camp, but here he was, sneering at her and Jonas.

"We'll be there soon," Jonas said, tightening the grip on her arm as they left the soldier behind. "This is not the right place to stop."

Nope, thought Janey. But was this even the right *time*? If Donaldson was still here, it meant the First World War was still going on.

Was she meant to be here? Seeing Donaldson and Jonas at the same time must mean that the last trip to the internment camp wasn't an accident. Or was it? Would she have gone to a different time if Max hadn't been holding on to her? Would Donaldson never have recognized her in this parade if she hadn't run into him with Max?

"Stop shaking your head. You're scaring the horse," Jonas muttered. Janey pulled herself together and waved carefully at the cheering crowds as the road climbed uphill.

"Every last Stoney Nakoda person must be in this parade," Janey said, peering around Jonas's headdress to see how far back the procession went.

"Almost. And from other bands too. Even up near Edmonton. Indian Days gives most of us a pass off the reserve."

"What do you mean, a pass off the reserve?"

Before Jonas could answer, a man in a buckskin jacket trotted past them on a cream-coloured horse.

"What have you got yourself there, Two Feathers?" He wasn't Indigenous, Janey noted.

"An old friend I didn't expect to see again," Jonas called after him, before the man sped on.

"Who's that?" Janey asked.

"Mr. Luxton. He organizes the parade. And pays us for coming."

At least there's that, Janey thought as they rounded a bend in the road. She gasped. The Banff Springs Hotel that rose into view didn't look like what she and Granny had pulled up to a few days ago. She blinked, closed her eyes and looked again. This was definitely the hotel, but a different, older – or younger – version of itself.

"Yup. Your people sure know how to build big," Jonas said.

The parade streamed into a courtyard, where hotel guests walked among the participants, stopping to examine a beautifully beaded saddle strap or coo over a Nakoda baby strapped to its mother's back.

Jonas guided his horse to one side of the courtyard, where Luxton was placing a bright red ribbon on a pony's bridle.

"First prize for this most charming travois," he said, and gave the woman something that quickly disappeared in the folds of her clothing. A decorated pole ran from each side of the pony's saddle to the ground behind it. A thick rug stretched across the end of the poles, where two toddlers, dressed in embroidered capes, sat patiently.

Jonas grunted. "Uh oh. Trouble at home tonight," he grumbled.

"Why?" Janey asked.

"Because Mary won for best travois."

"Your Mary? Your sister? That's Mary? But that's a good thing, isn't it?"

Jonas had already slid off his horse and held his arm up for Janey. "Not if your wife is in the competition too," he said.

Of course, thought Janey. Not only had the Two Feathers family grown older by at least 30 years, they'd also married, had families and...lived.

She approached the winner of the first prize and saw that the living hadn't been easy. The pretty young girl had somehow shrunk into this wrinkled, grey-haired woman with several missing teeth. But her smile, after the first look of disbelief, was wide and warm.

"The magpie with no sense has come back!" Mary said. She grabbed both of Janey's hands and studied her.

"Where did you find her, Jonas? Sitting in a fir tree?"

"No. Right next to the road. One moment there was nothing there, and the next this girl pops out from the crowd. At first I didn't believe it. But it's the same girl from that winter...looking kinda lost – like the last time. So I grabbed her. I knew you wanted to see her."

"You're not a magpie anymore. Your feathers have changed from blue and white to green," said Mary, eyeing Janey's long dress. She brushed one hand up Janey's arm. "I saw this when you slid from the horse," she said, circling the bite mark on Janey's shoulder with a calloused finger. "I left my mark on you," she said quietly. "But you left one on me too."

Janey remembered walking into Mary a couple of times as they traversed Sulphur Mountain, but she was sure she'd not left any marks. She eyed the woman again. Somewhere in the background, Luxton had stepped onto a balcony overlooking the courtyard and began to speak. But Mary and Jonas were still studying her. Janey realized her appearance must be as much of a shock for the Nakoda brother and sister as the time travelling was for her. Here they were, decades older, while she had only aged a day or two.

Behind Mary, the two little ones had lost interest in sitting on the travois and had climbed off.

"Your kids – I mean – your children?" Janey finally asked.

"These are my grandchildren," Mary said, a touch of pride in her voice. "I am Mrs. Hector Goodhunter now. I have two daughters and one son. These are my eldest daughter's children."

Janey stooped to say hello to the little girl and boy. They shied away, hiding behind their grandmother's skirts.

"There they are! Look! I knew it! They stole it or she stole it and bold as brass takes that grey horse and rides it down Banff Avenue rude as you please. Horse thief!"

Janey straightened to see Donaldson pushing through the crowd, a man in a bright red jacket in tow. She almost laughed. Here was a real, honest-to-goodness mounted police officer, Janey thought, but without the mount. Beside her, Jonas stiffened. Donaldson reached their little group and stood panting in the heat as he stared first at her, then at Jonas.

"I don' know which one of ya took it, but I want both of ya arrested 'cuz you're both trouble," he said, spitting out the last word.

"He says you stole this grey stallion," said the police officer, having finally caught up with Donaldson. His eyes slid past Janey to stare at Jonas.

"Wait a minute," Janey said, stepping between Jonas and the officer. "What horse are we talking about?"

"This one," hissed Donaldson. "The one that you an' your so-called cousin stole from me last spring. Or he did. Don' matter to me none, which one you arrest," he said to the officer. "All I know is that the last time I saw this horse, she was ridin' it and now they both are so that makes 'em both guilty. I spent days lookin' for that horse and nearly had to do time for losin' it."

Janey looked at the stallion. He had the same polished marble coat, she realized, as the one she and Max had ridden, but with a temperament so changed that she hadn't recognized him. While the horse rolled his eyes back from Donaldson's voice, he stood patiently as the toddlers played next to him. He must have escaped into a new life after he tossed her and Max from his back.

"Jonas Two Feathers had absolutely nothing to do with it," Janey said. "And this is a completely different horse from the one you put me and my cousin on. That one was skittish and barely rideable. This one's calm, except when *you* get too close." She pointed at Donaldson.

"What's going on here?" Luxton was gently elbowing his way through the crowd.

"He said –"

"They stole –"

"She's not –"

Even as angry words pecked at the air around them, Jonas Two Feathers and Mary Goodhunter said nothing. As Janey and the men argued, Mary tucked her grandchildren back onto the travois and headed the pony out of the courtyard. This gave Janey room to circle the stallion, which stood quietly behind Jonas, only skittering away slightly if Donaldson moved closer.

"Did you brand the horse when you had him?" she asked Donaldson.

"Naw. I was still tryin' to break it in."

"So you have no evidence that this horse belongs to you."

"I never said it belonged to me. It belongs to the internment camp. And you rode off on it."

"I think this little lady's right, Private," said Luxton.

Janey bit her tongue. She was neither little, nor this guy's idea of a lady, but she'd take support from wherever she could find it.

"It has a scar!" Donaldson said. "Under the saddle."

They stared at the horse. Because Jonas rode bareback, the stallion only had a decorative blanket slung across his back. The officer lifted the blanket. A cross-hatch of long white welts rose angrily from the horse's grey hide.

"There, see. I knew it. 'Cuz I was the one who –"

"Don't say it," Luxton said, looking at Donaldson as if the man had just peed in the street.

"Proves it though." Donaldson moved to take the reins.

The horse stepped back.

"Not sure that really proves anything," said Luxton, frowning. "Besides, isn't Mrs. Goodhunter's daughter racing this horse this afternoon?" Jonas nodded.

"Okay, how 'bout this," said Donaldson. "Let the horse race. If it wins, you keep it an' I won't say nuthin'. But if it loses, I take it. Fair and square. And I get to clear my name with the captain."

"Sir," said Luxton. "This horse has no brand. It is only your word. On the evidence of a whipping of the first sort, which no proper horseman – or soldier – would ever administer." He glared at Donaldson.

Donaldson pointed accusingly at Janey. "She knows it comes from the camp. Go on, tell him."

Before Janey could say anything, Jonas stepped in. "We agree to the terms of the race," he said.

"Are you sure, Two Feathers?" When Jonas nodded, Luxton went on. "Fine then. We'll see you all at the end of race. May the best man win."

Figures, thought Janey, watching Luxton and Donaldson disappear into the crowd. Even with Mary's daughter racing, it's still all about the best man winning.

Jonas readjusted the blanket on the stallion's back and, using the stone ledge of the courtyard, mounted the horse again. He pursed his lips at the ledge and looked at Janey, who was panicking at the thought of being left behind.

"Look, I'm sorry about your horse. And about Donaldson. And I hope your niece wins. But please don't leave me here."

Jonas grunted. "I can't pull you up on this horse again. Too old. So…"

Janey finally understood. She climbed on the ledge and then onto the horse. They picked their way through the courtyard, stopping only briefly for Jonas to chat with a middle-aged Nakoda woman who was readjusting the travois of a small, dappled pony.

"Who was that?" Janey asked as their horse moved downhill.

"The wife," Jonas said.

"Ah. The one that didn't win."

"I only have one wife."

"No I mean..." Janey changed the topic. "So where are we going? To the reserve?"

"To the camp. You still ask lots of questions." She could hear the amusement in his voice.

How else was she supposed to learn about things? "You guys still live in camps? That's great! So this Indian Days thing is a hunting break?"

Jonas snorted and pushed the horse to pick up its pace. They rode in silence for a few minutes, slowing again as several wagons carrying hotel guests all but blocked the road.

"We don't hunt much anymore," Jonas said, as they picked their way carefully along the side. When Janey glanced at him, his eyes were focused on something far in the distance.

"What do you mean, you don't hunt anymore? That's what your people...that's how you live." She studied the man, who seemed to be choosing and rejecting the words he wanted to use. He was silent until he guided the horse into the shade of a lane behind Banff's main street.

"The government says we hunted all the big game out of the park. Not enough left for the tourists to hunt. So my people must stay on the reserve. We cannot leave without passes. We cannot come into this park, except for Indian Days."

Janey was stunned. A whole group of people who had relied on hunting and gathering in the mountains for their existence was now reduced to living on a piddly patch of land? Mary – Mrs. Goodhunter – had been right. They'd been corralled into a box. Maybe it had open skies overhead and the mountains all around, but if you needed a pass to get out, it was still a box. How did this happen? She stewed for a while in silence, knowing that it was going to keep happening for decades after this Indian Days was over. She wished she knew why she was here. Because it wasn't to change the awful way the settlers who moved in had treated the people who were here first. She didn't have that kind of power.

"You'll get to meet the whole family at the camp," Jonas said, interrupting Janey's thoughts.

"Oh. That's great. Mary, I mean, Mrs. Goodhunter, she'll be there? And...your brother Peter?" She was a little worried about running into all that anger again.

"No," he said slowly. "You will not see Peter again. They arrested him for trespassing on park lands two years ago. In the fall. He was hunting deer for our family. They put him in jail. By spring he was dead."

"Oh." It came out as a tiny huff, the smallest of gasps, a soft little word that did nothing to stop the flood of shock and sadness that swept through her. Despite the heat of this high summer afternoon, Janey shivered and fought the urge to cry.

She wanted to give up. Nothing made any sense and she couldn't change or fix anything. The world was a colossal mess, and Janey couldn't do anything about it.

"Did you bring another trickster bag?" Jonas asked suddenly. "And some more candy?"

Janey roused herself from her black thoughts. "What are you talking about? What trickster bag?"

"The one like a window. But soft, like cotton. The one Peter threw in the fire."

The plastic zip bag! Full of jawbreakers! "No," said Janey, a smile breaking out despite her gloomy thoughts. "Did you find the candy?"

"Sure did. I don't know what was better, that bag or the candies in them."

"Well I'm glad you enjoyed them. Did your ankle heal all right?"

He nodded. "The bag is from another time, yes?"

Now it was Janey's turn to nod. She didn't know what else to say.

"We figured that, me and Mary. That's why I was only a little surprised when I saw you today. I nearly lassoed another girl; we're allowed to during the Indian Days parade. But when I saw you, I knew I had to take you. But I guess that meant Donaldson saw you and started with Four Winds."

Janey was confused. "Four Winds?"

"This horse. That's what our Grace calls him."

"And Grace is?"

"Mary's daughter."

Right. "How did Four Winds end up with you?" Janey asked.

"He...found the reserve."

"Maybe your Little People showed him the way," she said, smiling.

Jonas looked at her gravely. "He was in our pen at the

back of our cabin one day last spring. That's where Grace found him. She named him and trained him. I helped a little. That's why she let me ride him in the parade."

And now Grace might lose Four Winds if she didn't win the race. Great, thought Janey. Donaldson probably wouldn't have noticed the horse if she hadn't been on him. She was making everything worse. Could she just step off whatever time-travelling train this was, please, and grab the next one back into the 21st century? Was there a pine tree handy that she could fling herself into, or an embankment to slide down on?

Instead, they entered a large, flat meadow lined with colourful teepees near the base of Cascade Mountain. Nakoda women were packing away elaborate outfits and headdresses, while the men stood in groups, appraising a new horse or the quality of a pouch of tobacco. Children ran underfoot or chased the dogs that barked at the strangers wandering the grounds.

"Once a year, if we're allowed off the reserve, we can gather in this camp here in this field," Jonas said as they followed a wagon laden with crates and sacks. He eyed the contents critically. "Less this year than last year. Must be the war."

"Less what?" Janey asked, as the wagon slowed.

"Flour, tea, tobacco, sugar, potatoes, even beef."

The men on the wagon drove up to each teepee and handed out a portion of their goods. The quantity, Jonas explained, depended on the number of family members in the teepee. Before the wagon pulled away, the driver reached into a crate behind his seat and added a Bible to the stack.

"Before you white people came here, we had the land and you had the Bible. Now we have the Bible and you have the land," Jonas said, grinning. "Just don't tell my sister I said that."

He pulled up to a teepee adorned with green markings and helped Janey dismount. A girl rose from the shade of the shelter. She smiled at Janey, who was struck by how similar she looked to the long-ago Mary.

"Hello Uncle," she said, taking the reins.

"Hello Mouse," Jonas said, returning the girl's brilliant smile. "This is Janey. She's come to watch you win this afternoon. Or at least you better win." He turned to Janey. "This is Mary's youngest daughter, Grace."

She couldn't be more than 16, thought Janey. But she had the gentle, innocent smile of a girl much younger.

"Of course I'll win, Uncle. When I ride this horse, we are strong as the four winds," she said.

"No one's that strong, Mouse, but you need to win if you want to keep the horse," Jonas said.

A frown flickered across Grace's face. "But this horse –"

"Is a gift, Grace. Sometimes we keep our gifts, and sometimes we give them to someone else who needs them more," Mary Goodhunter said, having just arrived with the pony and her grandchildren.

"Does Janey need Four Winds?" Grace asked.

Janey shook her head vigorously. She didn't want to get in the middle of this. She had ridden the horse out of the internment camp, but he'd spooked and made his way to Grace, or Mouse, or whatever she was called. Four Winds belonged to her.

"Is there still some tea, Daughter?" Mary asked. When Grace nodded, the older woman urged the group to follow her behind the teepee where a kettle dangled over a tiny fire. She and Grace poured out mugs of strong, sweet tea and they settled into the teepee's shade.

"No more cooking with hot stones?" Janey asked.

"The kettle is easier. Harder to carry, but then, we don't travel much anymore," Mary said.

"Why is Janey here?" Grace asked.

Yes! For once someone else is asking the questions, thought Janey. Maybe she'll even get some answers.

"Because, dear child, I must thank her," Mary said. "She helped me protect you."

"How?" Grace asked. "I have not seen her before."

"No," Mary agreed. "Janey was here long before the Creator loaned you to us, my daughter." She ignored Grace's puzzled look and picked up the girl's hand, stroking it lightly.

"Our Grace came to me and my husband late in life," she said to Janey. "When she was born, she was so small, we called her Mouse." In the cool shade of the teepee, everyone smiled. "She was so small, we could hide her, even on the reserve. Even the Indian agent did not know she had come to be.

"At that time, many things were changing. Our other children had gone to the day school on the reserve, like me and Hector and Jonas before them. But they closed the day school. So the only school for our children was the orphanage. It was outside the reserve. For our children to learn, they would have to live there. In a residential school."

Mary paused to sip her tea, then continued. "'Try, somehow, to keep your children away from residential schools.' That's what you said. 'If you can, try to keep your children close.'

"Those were your last words before you left us. I remembered them. I told them to Hector, my husband. When it came time for our Mouse, we did not send her to that school.

We kept her close, at home. We hid her from the eyes that should not see her. We taught her English and Nakoda. And all of us, me and Hector, her aunties and uncles, her grandmothers and grandfathers, shared the old ways with her.

"One day we learned that they closed that orphanage outside the reserve, and they moved all those children to another school far, far away. Some of those children never came back to the reserve. But we," Mary paused to stroke her daughter's hand again. "We still have our Mouse. For this, I thank you."

Janey didn't know quite what to say. Could one desperate remark really change the life of Grace and those around her? Was it this easy? Was this why she was here? Janey watched as Grace jumped up and rushed off.

"It was nothing," she said finally. "Just a thing…I know… sort of."

Grace returned, the grey stallion in tow. "He *is* yours," she said, thrusting the reins at Janey.

"Oh no," Janey said, rising to her feet. "Four Winds doesn't belong to me. You need to keep him and race him this afternoon. And you need to win. Otherwise he'll go to a man who doesn't deserve him."

"We must go then," Mary said, gathering the mugs. "The others have already left for the bow and arrow contest."

They made it in time to see a row of men lined up, bows taut, on one side of the field. Someone released a sheep at the other end, smacking it on its rear to make it go. It ran, but not far, as a hail of arrows took it down. The crowd cheered wildly.

"How do they know who the winner is?" Janey asked.

"The one whose arrow is closest to its heart. But it

doesn't really matter," Mary said, nodding at the crowd. "They just want to watch us kill something with a bow and arrow."

She was moving them toward the edge of the meadow where horses and riders milled impatiently. Grace slipped onto Four Winds and cantered toward the group.

"You look after that horse, 'cuz it's goin' back with me," someone behind them shouted.

Janey turned to see Donaldson slouched against the side of a wagon, grinning at her. He'd removed the jacket of his uniform and rolled up the sleeves of his shirt.

"Go stuff yourself, Donaldson," Janey said.

"That ain't no way for a lady to talk, now is it?" he said, pushing off the wagon and limping toward her. "But then, if ya hang around with the likes of them Indians, ya can't really be a lady, now can ya?"

"Listen here you little piece of –"

"I'd love to chat, darlin', but I got me a race to watch," Donaldson said, turning abruptly and moving away from her. But he didn't go toward the bleachers at the side of the track. Janey watched him weave through the crowds and emerge at the far end of the meadow near a stand of trees. Odd, she thought, as she went with Mary toward the starting line.

Once again it was Luxton who introduced the riders and their horses to the crowd, explaining that the women would race first. "Some are as young as 15, some are grandmothers," he announced.

"That's our Grace he's talking about," Mary said proudly.

"Each race entails two completed laps around the meadow," Luxton went on. "May the best horse and rider win," he declared and fired his pistol.

Grace grabbed the lead right from the start. This'll be a

piece of cake, Janey thought, as the girl and the stallion flew down the track. "Go! Go!" Janey shouted, then turned eagerly to Mary. "She's got this. She'll keep the horse."

Mary didn't answer. She was watching the far end of the field. Janey followed her gaze and saw small flashes of light erupt from the side of the track, exactly where Donaldson had disappeared earlier. Janey took a step forward. No way could she run in these shoes, low-heeled or not. She pulled them off with one hand, hiked her dress up with the other and sprinted toward the flashing lights.

She was only halfway across the field as Grace and Four Winds approached the point where Donaldson hid. Janey hiked her skirt even higher to make her stride longer, but it didn't help. She watched as the light, which had been bouncing around the bushes, aimed straight for the horse's eyes.

Four Winds faltered, skittering away from the brightness, but Grace brought the animal under control and urged it forward. She glanced back only briefly, taking in the fact that Janey was running toward the trees, before the approach of the other horses spurred her on. Her lead was disappearing.

The last straggling horse had long passed when Janey reached the trees where Donaldson was hiding.

"You come out of there, Donaldson!"

"Hike your skirt up a little higher and maybe I will," he called back to her. "Threw me completely off my game, with ya runnin' around like that."

Janey quickly let her skirt drop back down to her ankles. "What are you doing in there? Come out and...and...fight like a man!" Wait, what was she saying? Had she lost her mind? What if he did?

The branch of a pine tree swayed and Donaldson's face appeared. "You come on over here and we can watch ourselves in this here lookin' glass," he said, and shone the reflected light of the sun straight into Janey's eyes.

"You spiteful piece of turd," she said, and hurled a shoe at him. Something splintered and Donaldson erupted in fury.

"Why you little..." He burst from the trees and barrelled toward Janey. Despite his limp, he could move. She flung the second shoe, but it bounced off him like a pebble off a charging grizzly. As Janey fled across the track toward the centre of the field, her feet tangled in the long skirt, tearing the fabric with every step, and making it easy for Donaldson to catch her in a tackle that knocked the wind out of her. "Let's see how uppity you really can get," he said, climbing on Janey's back so her face was pressed into the ground. Unable to breathe, Janey panicked.

"Get off her!"

Donaldson's weight shifted and Janey rolled over, gasping. Grace had Donaldson by the hair, yanking him back as Four Winds snorted and pranced around them, unsure of why he'd been heading for the finish line one minute, and into the middle of the field the next.

Janey rose unsteadily and stumbled toward them.

Donaldson twisted around and tried to grab at Grace. "Let go o' me, you dirty –"

"Shut up, shut up," Janey screamed, trying to pull Donaldson's grasping hands away.

"What's going on here? Pull yourself together man!" a voice commanded. Everyone froze. Luxton drew up beside them, jumped off his horse and hoisted Donaldson up by his suspenders.

"What on God's green earth gives you the right to fight a woman? No! Don't you dare," he warned, practically shaking the snide look off Donaldson's face. "I believe you owe these two young ladies an apology."

Donaldson seemed to take a moment to control his breathing. "She…an' her…" He pointed at the girls. "I didn't do nothin'," he said finally.

"He had a mirror and he was shining it in their eyes," Janey said.

"That's a bald-faced lie. I got nothin' in my pockets or in my hands."

Other people ran up. Jonas grabbed Four Winds' bridle and soothed the frightened horse, while another man in a suit tapped Luxton on the shoulder. "Sir, can we deal with this later? The winner is waiting for her prize."

Triumph slid across Donaldson's face. "So she didn't win, did she," he said, looking at Luxton.

Luxton hesitated, then grimaced. "No, it seems not. She saw you with this young lady and turned back to help her."

"Ha! I get the horse. Fair and square," Donaldson crowed, grabbing the reins from Jonas.

"But he can't. He –" Janey tried.

"I did nothin'," Donaldson snarled, turning back to her. "Ya threw somethin' at me and when I tried to stop ya from doin' it again, she turned around an' quit the race."

Mary approached the crowd, thrusting something into Janey's hands. She'd found Janey's shoes, but Janey was too angry to care.

"She didn't quit the race, you crapstick," Janey spat at Donaldson. "She…" She came back to help. Grace lost the race because of her. And she was going to lose Four Winds because of her.

Could Janey not do anything right? Just once, could she not have left well enough alone? If she'd only stood there quietly, Grace would have won the race. Four Winds was too fast and Donaldson too stupid to ruin the race with a mirror.

"Janey?" Grace put a hand on her arm. "It's all right."

No, it's not, Janey thought. Donaldson stood there gloating, while the others looked at her worriedly. Nothing was all right. But she didn't know how to fix any of it. All she did was make things worse. She turned away, desperate to hide from Grace's unearned forgiveness and from Donaldson's unbearable victory.

Shoes in hand, she stomped past the gawking crowds and across the field, not knowing or seeing where she was going because tears were pooling and threatening to run down her cheeks. If she kept walking, maybe she'd find out where she needed to be.

The thunder of approaching horses' hooves made her turn around.

"You can't get away this easy, missy," a voice shouted. She wiped her eyes. Donaldson was galloping toward her on Four Winds. Instinct made her run. She'd reached the first of the teepees before she felt the sting of a whip. Shocked, she nearly stopped running, but Donaldson was now beside her, his arm raised again. Janey didn't hesitate. She dove through the opening of the teepee nearest her and tumbled into a bottomless circle of black.

CHAPTER SEVEN

"There you are. We've been worried about you," Granny said, switching on the light. She did a double-take. "Goodness!" She approached Janey's bed warily. "I know you weren't keen on the dress, but did you have to kill it?"

Janey sat up groggily and looked at herself. Her dress was destroyed. The part of the skirt that wasn't ripped to shreds was smeared with dirt and grass stains, while her left shoulder was spattered with blood. She raised the sleeve, saw the slash from Donaldson's whip, and dropped it again before Granny could see.

"What on earth happened? I didn't see you in that little fracas on the dance floor. Did you fall? Are you hurt? Look at your feet! How did you get them so filthy? You look like you've run a barefoot marathon. What's going on?"

"I dunno, Granny," Janey said, pulling herself off her bed and into the bathroom, feeling as if she'd been body-slammed by a buffalo. She didn't want to think anymore or deal with Granny's questions, because she didn't have answers for anything or anyone. All she wanted was to clean herself off, crawl into bed and sleep until this was all over.

By the time Janey stepped out of the shower, her shoulder had stopped bleeding, but she put two bandages on it to keep it clean. It balanced the bite mark on the other shoulder, she thought, bundling herself into a thick hotel bathrobe. Her dress lay heaped on the floor. She'd deal with it tomorrow, she thought, nudging it into a corner with her foot until a flash of silver caught her eye. She bent down to pull Max's pin off the dress and read the inscription on the back again.

Funny how often she forgot to remember this pin.

Granny handed her a mug of hot chocolate as she entered the bedroom. "So, spill" she said. "What was Michael doing here? Did you invite him?"

This one, at least, Janey could answer. She sat down gingerly. "No. I didn't even know he was in Banff until I saw him on the ski hill today." Which felt like about a century ago, she thought, when you added in the time travelling.

Granny pursed her lips, then nodded. "It's not easy, is it, this life thing." You don't know the half of it, Janey thought. Her grandmother pushed a damp strand of hair from Janey's cheek.

The softness of her grandmother's touch contrasted so sharply with the sting of Donaldson's whip that Janey grabbed Granny's hand.

"Granny –" Everything felt so mixed up. Was she time-travelling to help Grace's family? She certainly wasn't doing a good job of it. She'd lost them the horse and drawn Donaldson's attention to the family. She'd felt a little sorry for the soldier after the first time she met him. After all, his brother had died in the trenches the previous year. So she could sort of understand his hatred of the inmates. But he'd been equally awful toward Jonas and Grace.

Janey shuddered, and then realized she was still holding her grandmother's hand. "Why are people so stupid when it comes to getting along?"

"I think it's all about fear, kiddo. Instead of looking at something new or different as a chance to learn, many people see something different as a threat to what they've always done."

A wave of tiredness washed over Janey. "But how do you fix that?"

Granny sat down beside Janey. "You can't fix the whole thing. But you can be kind. And willing to learn from the people you meet."

Despite the tears coursing inexplicably down her cheeks, Janey smiled. "And you can call out the people who aren't kind," she said, remembering the scene in the salon earlier that day.

Granny patted Janey's hand and stood. She began tidying Janey's side of the room. "On a completely unrelated topic," she said brusquely, "I have some good news. Your dad called. He has a new passport and they're trying to book the next possible flight out. It looks like we can all be together for Christmas."

"That's fantastic!" Janey brightened. "Let's pack so we'll be ready to leave tomorrow morning. We can meet them at the airport. Do you know when they're getting to Edmonton?"

"Oh kiddo, I'm way too tuckered to pack tonight. And they didn't have an arrival time. Because of the holidays, they're trying to piece together flights as they go, and the overseas flight will take at least seven or eight hours. But your dad sounded pretty sure they'll be here in time."

Granny hesitated, then sat down again. "Besides, Max still hasn't heard anything more about his dad and it's eating Charlie up. I can't even begin to think of what it's doing to Max."

She took Janey's hand again. "But I'm pretty sure that, despite a tussle or two on a dance floor, our being here is helping them deal with what has to be an unbearable situation. They've both lost so much already and I don't think we should run out on them until we absolutely have to. Could we wait until we at least know when your parents are landing?"

Janey looked away as a flush of guilt spread through her. Yeah, her life was complicated, what with the time travelling and the Michael thing and her parents being on another continent. But at least she *had* both her parents. Max only had one, and he was in danger. And Charlie, who'd already lost a daughter, now had to deal with a grandson who froze every time his phone rang.

Something else occurred to her as she looked at her grandmother's hand clasped around her own. All that whispering and hand-holding between Charlie and her grandmother? It might not be because they were into each other, though Janey kind of hoped it was. Really, Granny was probably trying to support a friend.

Janey could try too. She could be a bit kinder, but it would have to start tomorrow. Suddenly she could barely lift the mug of hot chocolate to her lips.

"Sure Granny, let's stay. As long as I don't have to go to another ball." She set her mug down carefully and burrowed under the soft duvet. She was asleep in seconds.

"Ah, Sleeping Beauty has arisen," Charlie announced from behind his newspaper when Janey cracked open the bedroom door the next morning. "We saved you some breakfast."

She wandered over to the trolley and checked under the silver covers. Fruit and yogurt under one, porridge under the other. With a shudder, she trapped the porridge back under its lid. Janey hated the stuff. She spooned fruit into a bowl and drizzled it with the yogurt.

"Any news about Max's dad?"

"Nothing yet."

Janey looked around the room, realizing it was just the two of them. "Where's Granny? And Max?"

"Amanda thought he needed a driving lesson in Marilyn to get his mind off things," Charlie said drily. "And even though he doesn't have a driver's licence, off they went."

"Ah. Well, it isn't the first time she's done something like that," Janey said, dropping into a stuffed armchair to enjoy her breakfast. Granny had let her take Marilyn along a deserted highway in the badlands of southern Alberta last summer. Driving through that surreal landscape, past hoodoos glowing with the setting of a prairie sun, was a memory that still made her smile.

"Yes. Your grandmother has some…uncommon ideas," Charlie said. He set the newspaper down. "And you have some uncommon friends. It added some excitement to last night's event. I'm sorry you had to miss the rest of the evening."

Not knowing what to say, Janey finished her bowl of yogurt.

"And I'm also sorry that Max was involved in that fight. It was uncalled for."

Michael hadn't been any better, Janey thought. What had been his problem? And it was Michael who started it. "I don't think Max was the one who –"

"No," Charlie said firmly. "Nothing is solved with fists and fights. I asked him to apologize."

Oh brother, she thought. She wondered whether Michael returned the apology, but she didn't want to ask. She rose from the couch. "I'm going to check out that heated outdoor pool. If Max gets back in the next little while, tell him to come down."

She stuffed her bathing suit into her pack and headed toward the elevator. It occurred to her that last night's fight wasn't the first time Max had used his fists. He'd punched Donaldson after the soldier had...what was the old-fashioned term for it? The elevator door opened and she stepped in, giggling. He'd "impugned her honour" by saying she was "giving it away". Janey snorted. Here she was, almost 15, and she'd never even kissed a guy. Not properly, anyhow. Still, it was funny how Max accused *her* of having a temper, and all the while he was ready to fight at the drop of a hat, or an insult. What was all that about?

Lost in thought, she stepped out when the elevator door opened and nearly knocked Max over.

"Whoops. Hello, dear," Granny said, after Janey and Max untangled themselves. "We've been out running errands. Max was saying that parking in Austria is so much easier with the smaller cars."

He wasn't saying anything now, Janey thought. He was staring at her as if she'd sprouted a horn or a massive pimple in the middle of her face. She pretended to brush a loose hair from her forehead. No weird bumps that she could feel.

"Really, it's okay Max," Granny said. "I have a guy at a body shop who can knock out small dings faster than you can say three-point turn."

Janey grinned at Max. "Did you hit something?"

"No, nothing that serious," Granny said, then stopped. Max still hadn't uttered a word. "Well," she went on as another elevator pinged open. "I'll take these parcels upstairs."

"We have to talk," Max said finally. "Come with me."

This should be interesting, Janey thought. He'd finally come around and realized that their trip to the internment camp had been real. It would be terrific to talk to someone who knew what was going on. Even if he'd only gone back once, he could help her figure out why she, or they, had travelled into the past. How were the trips connected? And how had she –

"Here is good," Max said, stopping in a quiet, empty little nook with comfortable chairs and writing tables. Before Janey had even picked out a place to sit, he began. "My grandfather says I must apologize," he spat out. "I am sorry. I am sorry I embarrassed you by fighting with your boyfriend."

"What? No. No, Michael's not my… Wait a minute. I thought you wanted to talk about what happened at the internment camp."

"Look." His eyes narrowed. "I am tired of all of this. I am tired of you. Of you saying things that are not true. Or forgetting to tell me things that are true. We went to the museum and that's all. You make things up. Or you tell me lies."

"Wait a minute. I do NOT make things up. I can't believe this. When did I lie to you?"

"Just now. You said Michael is not your boyfriend."

"He's NOT."

"Then why was he here last night? Why did he need to fight with me?"

"I don't know! Why did you fight with him? How do I know what goes on inside your tiny heads?" Her voice had risen so that the people walking by were glancing in. "You can go and stuff yourself."

She stormed out, unwilling to hear another word from him. But halfway along the corridor, she slowed and took a deep breath. The last time – no, times – she'd charged down a hallway and through a door, she'd been annoyed or mad at

Max and she'd ended up in the past. She needed to think. Maybe she could find the portal and not go through it. But which one? Carefully, she pushed open the door nearest to her. It opened into a broom closet. The next one was locked. Another one led into a kitchen. The doors were all intriguingly different, but none of them led into the past.

"Looking for something?" Sam had appeared at the end of the hallway.

"No, not really," she said, quickly letting go of another door handle. "I was wondering about all these doors, and why they're often so unusual."

"They seemed to put in a new style of door with each addition," he said as he glided toward her. "Have you seen the coffin doors yet?"

"Coffin doors?"

"Yup. Shaped like coffins. I'll show you. And it's on the way to the cookie-decorating workshop. You look like a person who could really use some coloured sprinkles."

Janey smiled and some of the tension inside her eased. Sam was right. Forget Max, forget time travelling, forget swimming. Decorating Christmas cookies was a fine idea. She needed to get herself back into the holiday spirit.

Sam led her up and down several sets of stairs until they came to a small, low hallway. He paused in front of a door – a coffin-shaped door. The pattern repeated all the way down the hall. "When vampires come to stay, this is where we put them," he said with a wink, before taking her through another corridor.

The scent of gingerbread greeted her even before Sam opened the door to the workshop room. He guided her to an empty spot at a table, then disappeared, returning with a cup of mulled cider and an apron. He placed them in front of her.

"Nathalie will bring the cookies to you personally," Sam said. "She's one of the pastry chefs here." He leaned closer. "In fact, she's our best pastry chef." As Nathalie arrived with a dozen gingerbread people carefully balanced on a tray, Janey caught the way Sam eyed the young woman. She was the one who'd been with Sam last night. Uh-huh. There was way more than the scent of gingerbread in the air.

"Ah yes. The girl who can waltz," Nathalie said, setting a dozen cookies on the table. "Great to meet you in calmer circumstances."

Before Janey could stop herself, the question that had nagged at her since last night popped out. "What actually happened? I, um, left halfway through."

Nathalie smiled. "Yeah, I remember seeing you rush out. I didn't blame you one bit. Sam and a few others pulled them apart and put the guy who wasn't staying at the hotel into a cab. The other guy...Charlie's grandson? He disappeared somewhere else in the hotel. But Mr. and Mrs. Claus stayed until the end."

"Thanks," Janey said awkwardly. "I don't know why they even started. It was all so stupid."

"You never know what will happen after a waltz," Nathalie said.

"Miss? Miss? Can you help me here? Lily, stop it!" At the next table, Ben was trying to wipe his little sister's hand, covered to the wrist with green icing, while she methodically dipped the wet fingers of her other hand into a bowl of chocolate sprinkles and popped them into her mouth.

"So much for calm," Nathalie said, rushing away with Sam.

Janey smiled, remembering her own early cookie-decorating days, including the time she tugged open the stopper of a glass tube, and shiny little pink and silver sugar balls exploded all over the kitchen floor. It had been like pulling the pin on a candy grenade. Her six-year-old self was delighted to learn that her socks could find the decorations even days later. When no one was looking, she'd pluck the little candies from between her toes to suck on until they dissolved.

The cider and the Christmas carols drifting from a nearby speaker soothed Janey. She would rise above Max's opinion of her. She would make a gingerbread person for him as well as for Granny and Charlie. Maybe a personalized cookie would help take Max's mind off things. It might even make him sweeter. She placed some gingerbread boys and girls in a row in front of her and began her task.

Charlie was easy: a Santa, complete with white trim and fluffy beard. She also made two for Granny, one with blond curly hair, turtleneck, jeans and dress boots, and another with a blond bun piled high, a red-and-white striped dress and red high heels – classic Granny. For fun, she took another gingerbread girl, changed the dress into a red cape and, using blue icing, outlined a girl in a super hero's costume. That one was for her. Janey would take whatever super powers she could find to survive these holidays.

She used more yellow icing to make the hair on Max's cookie and added blue dabs for eyes. Blue jeans, white shirt. Done. She still had a bunch of cookies left, and she'd bet that Max would probably eat more than one. Toying with the red icing that she'd used for Charlie's Santa, she painted a bright red kerchief around a gingerbread man's neck and added more blue eye dabs. Stefan, the young internee, was coming to life beneath her. By mucking several colours together, Janey produced a dull, dirty-grey icing that she painted on the Stefan cookie and the rest of the gingerbread men. She put down her tools and eyed the result.

"That's not a nice colour," Lily said. She'd crept up beside Janey, one finger in her mouth – probably loaded with more sprinkles, Janey thought.

"You're right, but it reminds me of some people," Janey said.

"They don't have any faces," Lily observed. "Not like these ones." Janey snatched Lily's wet, slobbery finger away from Granny's cookies. "I like these ones. 'Specially the stripey dress."

"Lily, we gotta go," her brother said, coming up behind her.

"Benny, look, they're all grey," Lily said. She snatched one and bit off a leg.

"Lily!" Ben cried, horrified.

"But they taste just as good as the coloury ones," Lily said earnestly.

Janey put a hand on Ben's arm. "Don't worry, it's okay," she said. "I have too many anyhow."

Ben yanked Lily away. "You know that Santa's watching you, don't you?" he scolded, dragging her from the room while balancing a boxful of their cookies.

Nathalie placed another box at Janey's elbow. "You can put your cookies in here when you're done," she said. She grinned wickedly. "You know, you probably have a direct line to Santa, who could mention a few things to Lily when she sees him. I sort of feel sorry for her brother."

Janey chuckled. "I'll let Santa know," she said, and began

packing away her creations.

"Those last ones do look a little grim," Nathalie said, nodding at the grey gingerbread men. "Is this a sort of post-modern, anti-Christmas statement? Or a case of colour mixing gone bad?"

"Not sure," Janey said, grabbing her pack. "But like the kid said, they still taste good." She waved goodbye, walked across the courtyard to the elevators and returned to the suite.

"Here she is, Alex. She's just walked in," Granny said, handing the phone to Janey. "It's your dad."

"Hi honey! I called to say we're about to get on the plane to Hong Kong."

"Dad! Hi! That's great! Is Mum with you?"

"Yup, do you want to talk to her? We haven't got much time, though."

"Sure. Just to say hi." And to find out if her mum, or her mum's family history, had something to do with her time travelling.

"Hi Janey! I can't wait to see you. Are you having fun swanning around in the Rockies?"

"Umm. Yeah. Hey, did our family have any kind of history here in the Rockies? Was someone from your side ever here, say, a long time ago?"

"What? No. Until we moved out there to join Granny two years ago, nobody from my side had been west of Ontario." Another dead end, Janey realized. But her mum cut off her thoughts.

"Janey, we've gotta go. They're boarding the last few people. We'll see you soon. Love you."

"Bye Mum." The click and then the dial tone at the end of a long-distance call had to be some of the saddest sounds ever, Janey thought.

"Glad to hear your parents are on their way," Charlie said. "And there's more good news. The detective has pinpointed an address near the Romanian border where she thinks Max's dad might be."

"That's fantastic," Janey said. "That's such great news for you," she added, looking at Max, who was working on his laptop. He glanced over briefly, but Janey noticed he was careful to avoid any kind of eye contact.

"Hey, these look like fun," Charlie said, opening the box of cookies she'd placed on the counter. "Did you make these, Janey? I can tell which one's mine. Look Max, this one has to be you." He was setting them all out in a row on the counter.

Max didn't bother looking up.

"What happened here? Did you run out of coloured icing?" Charlie had reached the grey gingerbread men. "And this one doesn't even have a leg."

"Oh yeah, Charlie," Janey said. "If Santa runs into a little girl named Lily, he should remind her that she shouldn't nibble on other people's cookies."

"He knows when you've been bad or good," Granny hummed, then stopped to pick up the cookie with the red-striped dress. "I'll take this one. C'mon, Max. Which one tickles your fancy?"

He sighed and got up. But when he saw the line of prisoner cookies, he froze. Ashen faced, he reached out to touch the gingerbread man with the red kerchief.

"This…this is…"

"Stefan," Janey said firmly.

He stared at them, frowning, then looked Janey squarely

in the face. "Yes."

Such a small word, Janey thought, as relief flooded through her. Three little letters to say that you agree and acknowledge and want to plunge into whatever the other person is offering. She held out her hand and, with only the slightest hesitation, Max took it. She pulled him toward the door.

"We forgot something downstairs," she called back to Granny and Charlie.

At the elevator, Max still looked a bit dazed. "That red scarf," he said. "As soon as I saw it, I knew this was not a dream. But still…"

"I know, I know, it's hard to understand," Janey said as the doors slid open and they stepped in. "The thing to figure out is why we went to the internment camp."

"And how," Max added.

He had a point, she thought. This morning's attempts to open doors in the hotel hadn't led anywhere.

"I thought I imagined our time in the internment camp," he went on. "They were prisoners; my dad is a prisoner. I just blended everything together. It felt so real, I thought I was going crazy. Even more crazy than when I was waiting in Vienna to hear about my dad."

"I don't think you're going crazy," Janey said as they reached the main floor. They stepped out and made their way along a hallway.

"No, not there," Janey said, pushing past the nook where Max had apologized to her before calling her a liar. They came to a room where a fire crackled cheerily in a large fireplace. "Here," she said, sinking into an overstuffed chair. Max took the one next to her.

Janey waited, sensing that Max was gathering his thoughts. "How many times have you gone back?" he finally asked.

Janey considered. "Since I've been here in Banff, three times."

"Always to the same place?"

"No. And that's what's so confusing." Words poured out of her as she outlined where she'd been and what had happened.

"But what do these things have to do with each other?" Max asked.

"That's just it," Janey said. "And how did I – we – get back there in the first place?"

Max made her go through exactly what she'd done each time she'd been transported back. "I don't know. I open a door and there I am," she said. "But I tried opening a bunch of doors this morning and nothing happened."

"Maybe you need a key," he said.

"Sure. Remind me to ask Sam to hand over the keys to this castle the next time we..." *Remind. Remember.* Wait a minute. A tingle of excitement shot through her and she had to stand.

"It's the pin! It's your pin! I had it with me each time I went back."

Max looked up at her. "My great-grandfather's pin? But why?"

Exactly, Janey wondered, collapsing back into the chair. Why would Max's family's pin be leading them into the past? She was pretty sure his family had nothing to do with hers, so why was she the one who was going back, with or without Max?

"Wait. Max, have you ever gone back without me?" Max shook his head no.

But Granny had said that Janey's dad's side of the family had never lived here, and her mum had confirmed the same on her side. What if the reason for time travelling had nothing to do with Janey and everything to do with Max?

"Tell me about the pin. How long has your family had it?"

He shrugged. "I don't know. My grandfather, the one with the horses, got it from his father. He gave it to mine, who gave it to me. That's all I know."

Another dead end. She mulled for a bit. "Okay," she said, "Let's forget that for a moment. What about the time you went back with me? What happened there?"

"Besides bullets flying past us and a horse almost taking us over a cliff?"

"Is that why we bailed?"

"Yes. I couldn't see where he wanted to go and I couldn't control him, so I thought it was safer to jump."

"He survived, you know," Janey said.

"Who?"

"The horse. Four Winds." Max looked at her blankly. "I saw the horse again, when I went back the last time."

Max nodded, but his mind was somewhere else. She wasn't about to tell him the whole story about Grace and the horse race. It seemed to have nothing to do with him or the pin.

"Do you know what Stefan told me?" Max asked suddenly.

"No. You guys were all speaking German."

"He's as old as I am, but they think he's 18," Max blurted out.

"Who?"

"The soldiers at the camp. It's a camp for men, but when they arrested his father, Stefan lied and told them he was 18 so he could go too."

"Why would Stefan want to go to an internment camp?"

"His father is, was, not strong, so Stefan went to look after him. They left his mother and his two sisters behind and he's worried about them. Their last letter said the bank took their farm. They wrote to say they were moving to Calgary to find work. But he hadn't heard from them in months. He wanted me to send them a message, to tell them that he and his father were still alright. But I didn't know how to explain what I was doing there." His voice trailed off.

Janey knew the feeling. If they could figure out what they were supposed to do there, then maybe things would become clear.

"Stefan said his family immigrated to this country 12 years before," Max went on, "when this country wanted settlers out west. Remember those posters at the museum? And then when the war started, they put these same people in internment camps. They even interned the ones who were trying to leave Canada so they wouldn't be arrested."

Janey was grateful there was no accusation in Max's words. "Yeah, it was truly crappy," she said. "What's worse is that we did it again in the Second World War with the Japanese. It's as if we didn't learn the first time."

"In Europe we didn't learn either," Max said quietly. "We had two world wars, all in my great-grandfather's lifetime! Crazy. He saw borders shift and people move from one country to another. One day their language or their religion or their nationality was okay, and the next, they were arrested for it, even murdered. How does this make sense? It's hopeless." He slumped forward in his armchair.

"I don't know, Max. I don't know how you make sense of that kind of evil." Janey wasn't sure how their conversation had gone from one young internee and his family to all the horrors of the world. Surely that wasn't why she and Max had travelled back through time. No way could she or Max stop the insanity of the reserves or the internment camps or any of the wars around the world. They were just two teenagers who wanted...what? The same as Stefan or Grace or Peter, to keep their families safe and together while global events swirled around them. What were she and Max supposed to do?

Max groaned. Looking at him, Janey realized that while he might be talking about the state of the world, what was really worrying him was his dad.

"He'll be all right, Max," she said softly.

"How do you know?" he asked fiercely. He stood and moved to a window, where sullen clouds puffed with snow had obscured the mountain peaks. Max looked out, his imagination focused on something else. "If they kill him, I'll..." He swallowed hard.

Janey thought desperately of something to take his mind off his father. "Tell me about your great-grandfather," she said. "What did he do after the war? Either war. Take your pick." She smiled wanly.

Max collected himself before he spoke. "He never talked about his childhood or his time during the wars," he began. "But he married and had two kids, my grandfather and my great-aunt Grazia." He stopped for a moment.

"After the second war, my great-grandfather raised

horses. Everyone thought he was crazy because he only raised grey ones. But not the performing Lipizzaner horses that Austria is so famous for."

The skin on Janey's neck prickled. "Wait a minute –" she began, but Max cut her off.

"Everyone thinks the Lipizzaner are all white, but true white horses have white skin under white hair, while our famous Lipizzaner have dark skins and white coats."

"No! Listen to me." Janey rose, grabbed Max and swung him around so that he faced her. "Why did your great-grandfather raise grey horses?"

Max stared at her for a half minute before answering. "Grandfather always said that a grey horse saved his father's life." The prickles spread to Janey's back. She pulled him toward the elevators.

"And what was your great-grandfather's name?" she asked urgently.

"Reiter, same as mine."

The elevator opened and they stepped inside. "No. I mean his first name?"

"I'm not sure," he said finally.

"How can you not –? Oh, never mind." She was trying to fit the pieces together.

"Why are we going back up?"

"To get the pin," Janey said, rushing to the suite as soon as the elevator slid open. "You need to get dressed. In warm clothes," she called over her shoulder. She'd been back in late fall, early spring and the height of summer. This trip, she was sure, would be in the dead of winter.

Granny looked up as she burst in. "Hey kiddo. Glad you're here. I need to ask you something."

"Can it wait? Max and I have something to do. Hi, Charlie." He nodded at her as she breezed past him toward the girls' bedroom.

"Any news?" Max asked Charlie. Janey paused to hear the answer.

"Nothing yet, son. I've just checked." Max disappeared into his bedroom.

Janey found the Banff pin on her bedside table and tucked it into her pocket, then grabbed her jacket and winter boots.

Granny came to the door of their room. "Janey! Stop for a minute. You need to hear this."

Janey froze. "What's the matter? Is it Mum and Dad?"

"No. They're fine. They've just taken off for Vancouver."

Janey pulled ski pants on over her jeans, fished out a scarf from her travel bag and tucked it inside her jacket. "So, what's the matter?"

"It's this weather. A storm is blowing in and if we don't leave within the next half-hour, we may be stuck here. Even with heavy-duty tires, Marilyn doesn't do waist-deep snow. We need to pack up and leave."

Again, Janey froze. Why? Why was this happening now, just when she was beginning to figure things out?

"Janey?"

She looked up. Max had joined Granny in the doorway. They were staring at her. "Any more news about your dad?" she asked.

Max shook his head. Janey found her tuque and mitts. "I think we should stay until we hear about Max's dad, Granny. I have a feeling it'll happen soon. After that, we'll sort out Christmas."

She kissed Granny's cheek as she left the room, took

Max's hand and headed toward the stairwell. They clattered down several flights of stairs before Janey picked a random floor.

"Whatever you do, don't let go," she said. She pushed open a door and they stepped into a blizzard.

CHAPTER EIGHT

"How do you do that?" Max asked, shouting above a wind that was whipping hard pellets of snow against their faces.

"I don't know. But I'm pretty sure it has something to do with your pin." Janey pulled on her hat and mitts. Max turned his back to the wind, flipped his jacket collar up and looked longingly at Janey's warm, fleecy accessories.

"Didn't I tell you to dress for the cold?" she snapped. He nodded, but this didn't dislodge the snow already building up in his hair. He looked frozen and lost. She pulled the scarf from inside her jacket and flung it over Max's head.

"What am I, your mother?" she grumbled, and then instantly regretted it. She really had to learn to think first. Max had no mother.

She stepped up to him, took the ends of the scarf and tied them gently around his neck. For the briefest instant, she felt the warmth of his breath on her cheek. She pulled away, but he caught her, and the thumb of his ungloved hand lightly caressed first her left eyelid, then her right.

"The snow, it collects on your eyelashes. Soon you will not be able to see," he said softly. While she could see just fine, she wasn't sure what she was looking at.

"I think –"

"What's going on here?" A voice, harsh and loud, forced its way through the swirling snow and pushed between them, so that Janey and Max sprang away from each other. Max peered through the snow. "Who is there?" he demanded.

"Oh no, it's not for you to be asking the questions," the

figure said, lumbering up toward them. "I ask the...well, for the love of all that is holy, why is it that I keep running into the likes of you?"

Janey's heart sank, but she lifted her chin. "Good day Private Donaldson." At least he wasn't carrying a whip. But he had a gun, probably the same one he'd used to shoot at fleeing prisoners. She reached for Max's hand and tried to pull him past the soldier.

"No, no, no, not so fast. Your type don't leave the warmth of your beds until about noon on days like this. What are you two doin' here this early on a February mornin'?"

Janey felt as if she was picking her way through landmines. Where was here? Were they back out at the internment camp? Were they in Banff? The wind shifted direction for an instant and Janey caught the whiff of sulphur. She almost smiled. Donaldson may have been part devil, but that rotten-egg smell meant they were near the Cave and Basin. "We wanted a peek at the hot springs," she said.

"Ha! The two of ya want to get to them damn aliens, don't ya? Never could understand why they had to move them into town last fall. Ya plannin' another escape for them? Not on my watch. I got that horse back an' I will do my damnedest to make sure nothin' else gets out. Now clear outta here." He fingered his gun meaningfully.

"We never helped anyone escape," Janey said hotly. Now it was Max's turn to tug at Janey's arm.

"Well you're certainly the master of it, aren't ya," Donaldson said. "Where'd ya go when ya vanished into that teepee?"

"I don't need to answer any of your questions," Janey said. She turned and stalked downhill, hoping she was heading toward the Banff town site and praying Donaldson wouldn't shoot them in the back.

"Yeah, that's right. Keep on goin'. I'm watchin' you two. 'Cousins', my ass." His voice faded as Janey strode on, determined to leave him behind and put as much distance between them as possible. But it was hard to march away haughtily when the footing was so treacherous. A wrong step on a patch of ice sent her arms flying up to grab a handhold.

"Are you okay?" Max asked.

"Yeah, sure. Hey, look at this." They peered at what had stopped her from sliding down the path. A wooden crutch, battered and split, was nailed to the trunk of a tree. Snow was settling along the length of a child-sized one below it.

"Here's one more! And a cane," Max called out. He'd moved down the trail. The more they looked, the more crutches and canes they found propped or nailed to trees.

"This must be from the people who think they're cured at the hot springs," Max said. "There's something like this at Lourdes in France. There the people think the water is holy and can heal them, and they even leave wheelchairs behind."

"Huh. Well to me, the spring water is just hot and smelly," Janey said, making her way carefully along the path. "People must have figured that out over the last hundred years, because they don't leave all this stuff behind now."

They reached the bridge that she and Jonas had crossed on Four Winds. Was it only yesterday? Or the previous summer? Or the previous century? The confusion – and the cold – was making her head ache.

"Some people would say all water is holy," Max said.

They might be right, thought Janey. The river under the bridge was a smooth, frozen sheet of white. But underneath that snow and ice, water was still coursing down from the mountain glaciers toward the centre of the continent and all the people who needed it to survive.

"Janey, wait," Max said, as they reached the other bank. She stopped to face him. "What are we doing here?"

"Is this one of those big philosophical questions about life?" she asked. He stared at her silently until she looked away. The snow had stopped, and she could see down along Banff's main avenue. People were emerging onto the street, clearing walks or dashing into other buildings. "I'm not sure," she said finally. "I think it has something to do with Stefan. I think we have to help him and his father get away."

"You're as crazy as that soldier. He will shoot us if we go near the prisoners. And we don't even know where they are."

"Look behind you, Max."

He turned and they watched as several straggly columns of men stumbled along the path toward the bridge. A grey horse pranced around them, its rider urging the dishevelled group to pick up its pace. "The faster ya go, the warmer ya'll be," the rider called.

"It's Donaldson again," Max said grimly. "And he has the horse we rode on the last time."

"Now there's a surprise," Janey said wryly. They moved briskly past several buildings, ducking between a storefront and a cabin.

"Before anything else, we need to find out if Stefan is even here," Janey said.

"I agree. But couldn't we find somewhere warmer?" Max was shivering, despite her scarf.

"Let's wait. I want to see where they go."

The horse and the prisoners straggled toward them. Even

from here they could see that Four Winds resented his rider. Donaldson's whip was out.

"There, look," Max said, and Janey followed his gaze to a slight young man in an oversized coat belted at the waist with a thick rope. A flash of red peeked out from above his upturned collar. He looked neither left nor right, only concentrating on placing his shoddily clad feet into the footsteps of the man in front of him.

Max and Janey gave the group lots of time to move down the avenue before they stepped out and followed. Several blocks down, the prisoners halted in front of a huge white building set up, inexplicably, in the middle of the street. It glistened in the emerging sunlight.

Janey stopped in awe. "It's all made of ice, with a turret on it, of all things."

"Indeed, this is our new ice palace. It's being built for our inaugural winter carnival," said a man who'd stopped next to them to admire the construction. "I believe that is what one calls a tower, as turrets are usually circular in design, and this one is square."

Janey glanced at the man, eyebrow raised at all this information. "Sorry to be such a pedant," he went on, "but words are important. I'm Luxton, by the way. Are you visiting our fine town for the carnival?"

She looked more closely. "Did you…were you…" She gathered her thoughts. "You were at the Indian Days horse races," she finally said.

"Wouldn't miss them," Luxton said. "Were you there as well?"

Janey shivered. "Yes. I was there when Grace raced her horse and…and…lost it."

Luxton peered at her closely. "You're that young lady!" He stepped back to take her in properly. "And here I thought you were just a couple of fellas in early to see what Banff has to offer in the winter." He scratched his head. "You're Janey. And I know someone who wants to see you. Come along. That cold-looking young man beside you should come too. We'll warm him up." He turned off the main avenue onto Caribou Street.

Max pulled her back. "What about Stefan?" he hissed.

"I don't think we can snatch him off that tower right now," Janey said, nodding at the ice palace now swarming with internees. Some were cutting ice blocks, while others were hoisting them up the wall. At the top, Stefan was hammering a long stake into the tower. "Let's find out what we can. Maybe he'll be down on solid ground by the time we have a plan."

They caught up with Luxton halfway down the block. "Mind the toboggan run," he said. "We're testing it this afternoon. It starts up at Tunnel Mountain and runs for a mile straight through town to the Bow River."

"Why is it called Tunnel Mountain?" Janey asked. This had puzzled her since she'd arrived in Banff. "Is there a tunnel under it?"

Luxton snorted. "No. The CPR surveyors wanted to build a tunnel straight through it for the railroad." He steered them onto Bear Street. "But Van Horne put his foot down. Too much money. They found a much less expensive route just north of here."

"So they named it after a tunnel that doesn't exist?" Janey asked.

Luxton pushed open the door of a small, square log cabin.

"It could also be considered a reminder to think things through," he said. "Please step inside. I believe there's someone here to see you."

A small girl rushed up. "Papa!" She flung herself into Luxton's arms.

"Hello dear, did you write my editorial while I was gone?"

"No Papa. But I think it should be about the winter carnival. Is the maze finished yet?"

"Not yet, my dear, but they're getting ready to put the flags on the ice palace. We'll have a good look after our dinner."

A taller girl, wrapped in shawls, stepped out of the shadows.

"Ah, Grace. Look, I've brought you even more than this pass for your family," Luxton said, handing the girl a thick envelope.

"Grace!" Janey stepped forward. She wanted to hug the Nakoda girl, but guilt held her back. "I never told you how sorry I was that I made you lose your horse."

Grace's broad smile warmed the room even more than the wood-burning stove at its centre.

"Four Winds is still among us. I saw him this morning. But you! I am so happy you are here." She flung her arms around Janey's neck and they hugged.

"Who are these people, Papa?"

"This is Janey, whom I met last summer, and this is..." Luxton turned to Max, at a loss.

"And this is my cousin, Max. He's here...visiting with me," Janey said.

"Ah," Luxton said. "And this is my daughter, Eleanor. Welcome to the office of the *Crag & Canyon*."

"Why is that lady wearing trousers, Papa?"

Luxton looked perplexed. Janey crouched down so she was eye level with the girl. "Where I come from, this is the latest in winter fashion," she said. "It's easier to do sports, and it's much warmer than skirts."

"But you still look cold," Eleanor said. "Should we get them some tea, Papa?" He nodded. She and Grace gathered mugs and spoons while Luxton checked out a page of closely set type.

"Now I see why you think words are important," Janey said. "You run this newspaper."

"Norman Luxton, editor, at your service," he said with a mock bow. "What would you like to know? How many events we'll have? What the ski jumping entails? Where the teepee pitching will be?"

"Actually, I'd like to know where the internees live," Janey said, gratefully accepting a mug of hot, sweet tea from Grace.

"Why?" Luxton's voice grew reserved.

"Well, I'm interested in them and why they're here."

"They're here because most of our able-bodied young men are overseas fighting for king and country," Luxton said.

"The internees don't want to be here in a camp," Janey said quietly, not wanting to upset the man whose tea she was drinking, but not willing to back down either.

"No. And most of our young men don't want to be fighting overseas."

"And Grace's relatives don't want to be stuck on the reserve," she shot back. "Now they need a pass to get off their reserve to go onto land they used to roam freely."

Luxton pursed his lips, then sighed. "Yes," he said finally. "We appear to have an infinite capacity for dividing people into those who can and those who can't."

Before Janey could say more, Grace tugged at her sleeve. "Come see my horse before I go," she said. "She is not as fast as Four Winds, but she has a heart shape on her head. I call her Hope. Max should come too."

Once the door to the newspaper office clicked shut behind them, Max turned to Janey. "But we didn't find out where the internees stay."

"They live in a camp beside the hot springs," Grace said. "Mama says it's like our reserve, only they can have a hot bath in the winter. But I know where they are now."

"So do we. We also saw them at the ice palace."

"No, now they are at the stables, I am sure. They eat their dinner there. And that is where my horse is."

She led them several blocks past a large hotel to a wooden stable behind it. The trio stepped around several piles of steaming manure, pushed open the stable door and entered. As her eyes adjusted, Janey picked out about ten men sprawled on hay bales or crouching on the floor. They looked up suspiciously, guarding the bread in their hands. Only the soft whicker of horses from the stalls in a room behind them broke the stable's silence.

"Is Stefan here?" Janey's question dropped into the middle of the workroom, which smelled way worse than the manure outside. The men turned back to their dinners, saying nothing.

"Let's go see her horse, Max," Janey finally said.

"Max?" A voice, hoarse and raw, crept out from the corner of the stable where several men were huddled together.

"Yes, I am Max."

One of the figures rose stiffly and moved toward them.

"Did you speak with my mother?" Stefan stood before them, taller than the last time, but thinner and...greyer. Dark circles smudged the contours under his eyes, which looked beaten and sad.

"No," Max said. "I have not been to Calgary yet."

Stefan looked at him bleakly. "It is better so," he said finally and looked down.

Another man came up, put his hand protectively on Stefan's shoulder and whispered something. Stefan shook his head. The man tried to pull the boy back into the corner. "Go away," he said to Max in a thick Ukrainian accent.

Max was puzzled. "Why Stefan? What's wrong? And where is your father?"

Stefan gently shook the man loose. "They took my father to hospital. But too late. He was too sick. He died. Three weeks ago." Max's face went white. He muttered something in German and Stefan nodded miserably.

Max rounded on Janey. "So. We have found him. Now what?"

"Hang on a minute," Janey said. She didn't exactly have a plan.

"I don't think we have that much time," Max replied. The cold had taken hold of him again and he shivered as he peered through a gap in the boards of the stable wall. "That's Donaldson out there. He's the one smoking a cigarette."

Moving only on instinct, Janey grabbed Max and Stefan and pushed them toward the stalls, closing the door to the workroom behind them. Grace was saddling up a small, chestnut horse.

"Look, Janey, here's my new horse, Hope. And here, in the next stall, is my old horse, Four Winds." Delighted, she swung open the stallion's stall door so they could say hello properly. Four Winds nickered softly, especially at Stefan's touch.

Janey approached Grace's new horse. "She's beautiful," Janey said, taking in the distinctive white heart on the mare's forehead. She turned back to Grace. "I have to ask you something, and you can say no," she began.

Max pushed aside an old wolfskin nailed to the wall to peer through another gap in the boards. "He's almost finished the cigarette," he whispered. "We don't have much time."

"Grace –" Janey stopped. Was it fair to put the girl in harm's way?

"Janey! We must do something."

"Can you take our friend Stefan away from here? He needs to get to Calgary."

Grace smiled. "Yes. Easy. I will take him to the reserve. Then we will find him a way to the city."

Janey hugged her. "Can you go now? We'll make sure Donaldson doesn't see you leave."

Grace nodded, mounted her horse and held out her hand to Stefan. He looked bewildered. "Go with her, please," Max urged and helped him up.

Behind them, they heard the door into the workroom swing open. "On your feet, ya garlic eaters. Enough lazin' around."

Max darted to the opposite wall and pulled open a large door. "Don't let him catch you," Janey said. Grace smiled again, trotted through the door and broke into a canter as soon as they were out of the yard.

From behind, they could hear Donaldson giving orders. "I need six of ya to finish cutting the ice blocks," he said.

"And stop being such lazy sons of dogs!" The sickening sound of a boot driving into a body made Janey want to storm back into the workroom.

Instead, Max dragged her over to Four Winds. "The other horse is slow. We must take this one from Donaldson."

"Can we ride right over him and grind him into the pavement?" Janey muttered. She pulled the wolfskin off the wall, mounted behind Max and wrapped it around him. "This'll help you stay warm."

Donaldson's voice shot out again. "Wait, I'm short a Hun. Where is he? Hidin' out with the horses again?" Donaldson burst through the workroom door, just as Janey, Max and Four Winds stepped out of the stable.

Janey twisted back, unable to resist. "Hey Donaldson! We have Stefan. And you have turds for brains."

A shot whizzed past them. They galloped out of the courtyard, down a lane and along a back road. Janey had no idea of where they were going or where Stefan and Grace had headed. Getting out of the range of Donaldson's gun was probably the first order of the day. As they rode toward the edge of town, the buildings grew sparser and offered less cover. Their path though, was heavily travelled, which meant their tracks would be hard to follow. She settled in behind Max, clinging to his tight, lean frame as much for comfort as for warmth. That bullet had unnerved her. If Donaldson shot again, she'd be the first one down.

In the tangle of trees at the side of the path, a flash of chestnut caught her eye.

"Max! Wait!" Janey shouted into his ear.

"What?! We have to get away."

"I know, but I think we passed Grace and Stefan. They're

going too slowly. We have to turn around."

She felt, more than saw, his shoulders sag. But he tugged gently on the reins and Four Winds responded instantly. A half minute later they were back where Janey thought she'd seen the chestnut horse. She studied the brush carefully.

"There. I knew it." The hoofprints led in behind some fir trees. They picked their way along the path through scrubby forest. Only five minutes in, they found Grace and Stefan leading a hobbled Hope behind them. Grace beamed when she saw them.

"You are not the angry soldier," she said delightedly.

"No, but what happened to Hope?" Janey asked.

"Her leg. We were too close –"

"I fell off the horse," Stefan said miserably. "To get on again, I pushed her against a gate with a big nail in it. I did not see it."

A tightly wrapped strip of cloth around Hope's hind leg bloomed red.

Would anything go right for them, Janey wondered. Which was exactly when Four Winds raised his head attentively. Half a second later they heard the thrum of horses heading toward them.

Janey grabbed Four Wind's reins and thrust them to Grace. "Take him," she said. "Get Stefan out of here."

Grace, who'd been listening attentively, shook her head. "No. They are three horses now. Three horses with three riders will find us. We must…" She considered. "The buffalo. They will help us. Set them free. The ones in the paddock. Use the wolfskin. And we will go to Sleeping Buffalo. You will bring Four Winds there."

"Wait. Where is this paddock? And where is Sleeping

Buffalo?" The hoofbeats of their pursuers shook the air around them, and Janey prayed they were far enough off the path to be properly hidden. And what was she supposed to do with the wolfskin?

"The paddock is just ahead," Grace said. "And Sleeping Buffalo is our name for Tunnel Mountain. We will wait for you there. Go."

Janey and Max mounted Four Winds again and headed in the direction Grace had indicated. Five minutes later they reached the edge of a large, open, fenced area dotted with huge shaggy beasts that stood impassively in the cold. At the same moment, three riders pulled up by the gate on the other side of the paddock, their horses panting and snorting as they wheeled around in the cold.

"Not sure they went this way, Donaldson," one man shouted.

"I saw 'em, all three o' them, escape on that grey stallion. I want 'em back!" Donaldson shrieked, staring blindly at the landscape around him.

Janey took in the pursuers, the buffalo, the gate and the wolfskin draped over Max's shoulders. She knew what Grace wanted her to do.

"I need that fur," Janey hissed.

"What? You have more warm clothes than I do," Max grumbled.

"And your jacket. Give it to me. And then move back so you're really hidden."

She was on the ground, her own jacket already off. Max reluctantly gave her his and the wolfskin. Janey squeezed through a break in the fence and took a deep breath.

From here, the buffalo looked like huge, overweight cows.

Janey wasn't fond of cows. "Don't think about it," she told herself, pulling the wolfskin over her head. "Just do it."

She crept toward the beasts, keeping them between her and the men at the gate, and raised her arms, a jacket in each hand. Would this work? Every kid who spent any time in the Rockies knew not to approach the wildlife. What was she doing?

The men's voices grew louder. They were arguing. Would this scare the bison away from the gate? The buffalo closest to her raised its head and eyed her suspiciously. Please, please don't come this way, she prayed. She lunged at it and it turned, nudging another creature away from her too. Keep going, keep going, she thought. Crouching, Janey shook the jackets at another buffalo, and it too, turned and followed. Other animals looked up and Janey ran toward them, keeping close to the ground. Fear coursed through her body, urging her forwards, pulling her backwards. Despite the cold, a prickly sweat sheathed her skin and she panted, low and hard, like the wolf that had lived and hunted in the skin she now wore.

Clumsy and lumbering, the buffalo picked up speed, moving as one in a massive, rumbling river toward the gate. Janey's fear dissolved and elation took hold, pushing her onward. She had them now and they were all running, thundering toward the flimsy entrance of the paddock.

All of them, but one.

It stood, tail twitching, staring Janey down. She stopped, crouched low, then skittered to one side; her world narrowed to the tiny space between her and the enormous creature in front of her. And then it charged.

Janey turned and ran back to the paddock fence, knowing

she would not make it over, but not knowing what else to do.

Max galloped toward her. "Take my arm!" He leaned over the fence and Janey grabbed hold. Four Winds reared up and Janey rose, up, over the rails, the hot, fetid breath of the buffalo whirling around her as it snorted and veered from the barrier at the last possible moment Sobbing, she dropped sideways onto the saddle in front of Max. He wrestled to control the horse, which had been equally terrorized by the buffalo's charge.

"It's all right," he said, soothing them both, one arm around Janey, the other patting the horse. "You're safe. Shhh."

Janey wiped her eyes. "I'm sorry. Thank you. I –" She stared at him. Somewhere behind her, the sound of stampeding animals, splintering fences and angry men ricocheted through the winter air. It didn't matter. She was safe. Max had pulled her out of harm's way. The world quieted for just an instant.

Impulsively, Janey pulled his face toward hers and kissed him. His lips were soft and gentle and…hold on… What was she doing? She pulled away. "Oh god. I should have asked you. Is it okay to kiss you?"

Max grinned, cupped her cheek and kissed her back, a more forceful embrace that left her feeling dizzy and breathless. Who knew how long the kiss would have lasted, if it hadn't been for the gunshot that echoed through the valley? The sound startled Four Winds, and Max and Janey pulled apart as the horse moved away from the noise. Janey peered over Max's shoulder.

"It's Donaldson. He's coming this way."

"Where are the other two riders?"

Janey scanned the far side of the paddock. "One guy's lost

his horse, and the other one's chasing the buffalo."

"Get into the saddle. We have to move."

Janey slid her right leg over the stirrup so she faced forward and they galloped back toward the woods. Inside the trees, Max reined the horse in so they could put on their jackets. But even after they'd dressed, he guided Four Winds uphill through the underbrush at a pace Janey found far too slow.

"Can't we go any faster?" she asked.

"I am sure the horse Donaldson has is slower than Four Winds. Also, I can't see what's under this snow and I don't want Four Winds to be hurt. Stefan and Grace need a horse that is not lame."

Good point, Janey thought. She should concentrate on getting Four Winds to them and not on what had happened back there. Because that was...well, what? It was a kiss, and it was with Max, and not with Michael. And it was her first kiss. Was this –

"How did you learn to do that?" Max asked.

"What? Kiss? I didn't...I mean, I don't do it...I mean –"

"No. With the buffalo. Scaring them like that."

Fine. They weren't going to discuss the kiss. "The people of the plains used to hunt buffalo this way long ago, before they had guns and horses. They'd stampede them right off cliffs. They probably did a way better job of it than me. I bet they didn't have bulls turning on them."

The slope was growing steeper. She could feel Max leaning forward against her. Should they talk about what happened back there? Did the kiss mean anything? Or was it just a –

"Look." Max pulled to a stop and pointed at the ground. A set of horse tracks led one way, while two sets of human footprints went another. "I think we follow the people," he said. Ten minutes later, they found Stefan and Grace.

"Hope will find her way home without us," Grace explained as Janey and Max dismounted. "And maybe the soldier will not understand the tracks."

"Grace, thank you so much for doing this. And please, be careful," Janey urged. As Grace mounted, Janey turned to Stefan. "And you, take this." She pulled Max's pin out of her pocket and placed it carefully in his hand. "Whatever you do, don't lose it. And when you are safe, give it to someone who needs the strength of these mountains. Don't keep it. Promise me."

He nodded. In the light of the afternoon sun, Janey realized that the winter-sky blue of Max's eyes was reflected in Stefan's. "Thank you," he said.

Max and Stefan hugged briefly. *"Vergiss mich nicht,"* they both said. Even their voices sounded the same, Janey thought. As Stefan mounted, Max handed him the wolfskin.

"Hey Stefan," Janey called. "What's your family name?"

"Reiter," Stefan replied. Max gaped. Janey only nodded and smacked Four Winds gently on the rump.

"But...but that is my name," Max said as the grey horse disappeared up the trail.

"Yes," Janey said. "He's your great-grandfather."

"But how did you know?"

"I wasn't sure," she said, doubling back down the track. "But I couldn't figure out why else we were travelling into the past."

Max digested this as they headed downhill, away from Grace and Stefan. "If he is my great-grandfather, that means he will escape. But he will go back to Austria."

"Yes, where he'll raise horses and a family and eventually you'll come into the world."

"But why did you tell him to give the pin away? This way it's gone from our family."

"I had to break –"

This time the gunshot didn't echo around the valley, mostly because the bullet took out a chunk of the aspen tree next to them before lodging in a fir.

"I said stop. Ya horse-thievin', prisoner-snatchin' traitors. What've you done with that lazy Hun? I knew I shoulda shot you two the first time I saw you. Ya arrogant, war-dodgin' slackers. Ya stole a prisoner and made me lame my horse. This is it. I'm gonna arrest ya or shoot ya dead." Donaldson fired again and cursed when he missed. Waving his gun, he staggered toward them.

Max and Janey pushed on, plowing through the knee-deep snow, aware that they were making it easier for Donaldson to follow and unsure of what to do other than keep moving. Not daring to check behind them, they slipped and stumbled along, dodging trees and Donaldson's fury.

At least he was on foot too, and his limp wouldn't help him. Janey wondered if Donaldson had lamed his horse by riding it too quickly up the mountain. His loss, their gain. She looked up from the path they were creating, trying to orient herself.

"There. Look," she panted. In a clearing ahead of them, a mini-mountain of snow rose over their heads. Steps were carved into one side of the snow pile, and a wooden sled leaned against the other. When they reached the sled, Max grabbed it and dashed up the stairs. It nearly flew from his hands as another bullet struck it. Janey ducked behind the stairs while Max, at the top of the pile, stood stunned and exposed. Donaldson was close enough that Janey heard him cock his gun. Another click, and then Donaldson swore.

"Hurry Janey! His bullets are finished."

Janey dashed up the stairs. Max was already on the sled. She flung herself on top of him.

"Don't you dare! Stop now!" Donaldson called.

"Go," Janey commanded, wrapping her arms around Max for the second time that day. He pushed off and they plummeted down the hill, the wind whistling past their ears and muffling Donaldson's shrieks. The toboggan run dipped, then rose and for an instant they were airborne, a terrified, eight-limbed bird with two frantically beating hearts, before the sled thumped down onto the run again and shot around a bend.

Now they were zooming through the town, onlookers gaping and pointing. A woman dragged a child out of the way from where he stood, open-mouthed, in their path. They flew past Grizzly and Muskrat Streets, across Banff Avenue, over Bear and Lynx Street, and hurtled onto the Bow River, all ice and snow, toward the opposite bank, where their ride ended in an explosion of cold, white oblivion.

CHAPTER NINE

Janey gasped, inadvertently sucking in some of the snow swirling in sheets around them. She closed her mouth, swiped her face and sat up. She could barely see through the blizzard. Where was Max? And where was Donaldson?

Someone grabbed her arm and Janey reared back. "It's me. It's only me." Max was trying to pull her to her feet.

Thankful, Janey rose. "Have you seen him?" she asked anxiously.

"Who, me?" A figure floated toward them. "We really need to put more sand on the sidewalk in weather like this," Sam said.

They'd done it! They were back in the present! Janey was so relieved that she wanted to lie back quietly in the snow and just...think for a minute.

"Here, let me help," Sam said, grabbing Janey's other arm and steering them back to the hotel. "I'm glad I found you. There's a guy in a red suit who really, really wants to talk to you."

"No. Wait." Max stopped in the path and tugged at Janey's arm.

"Max," she said, "I think your grandfather has some good news for you."

"Exactly," said Sam. "Let me take you to him. He's in Mount Stephen Hall and I know a shortcut."

They rushed through a door and along several corridors before coming to a grand, timbered hall festooned with pine and poinsettia garlands over each archway. Lights from the candelabras and a massive Christmas tree heightened the warm glow of the Tyndall stone walls. Looking up, Janey took in the second-floor gallery lining one wall, where that odd painting with the backward signature hung. Was it only three days ago that Ben had shown her the painting?

The hall teemed with excited children waiting to say goodbye to this genuinely jolly Santa. No wonder Charlie was in such great demand, Janey thought, watching from the sidelines. He looked truly, joyfully happy. Even Max held back, not wishing to pull Santa's attention away from the little ones.

"Ah, Lily," Charlie said, smiling down at the impish girl who had planted herself in front of him. "Did you like those gingerbread cookies this morning? Even Janey's?" Lily's eyes grew wide and she backed up, stepping squarely on her brother's toes. Ben grimaced but said nothing. Charlie chuckled. "They're my favourite too," he said, and winked at her. "And Ben, you're being a terrific big brother. Good for you!"

Ben blushed and tugged his dazed sister away. Glancing after them, Charlie caught sight of Max and Janey.

"Max! Dear, dear boy! And Janey!" He swept them into a bear hug. "Such news. Come with me." He urged them into a quiet corner, pulled his un-Santa-like phone from his jacket pocket and thrust it at his grandson. "They've found him," he said excitedly. "They've found your father! They called about 20 minutes ago. He's safe, fine. Here. He's waiting for your call."

Max stared at his grandfather, frozen in place, unable to believe the good news. "Take the phone and look at the last caller," Janey said, pushing him toward a quiet hallway. Hands trembling, he fumbled with the keypad. "Here," said Janey, and found the right buttons.

"Papa!" she heard Max say before his voice choked up. She patted his shoulder, then left him to talk to his dad in private, all of his worries finally laid to rest. Janey was happy for him. He'd go back to Austria and his gymnasium and his Latin classes, and his life would be normal again.

At the entrance to the large timbered hall, she paused. Just inside, a small boy had cornered Charlie and was earnestly explaining why his friend Abdullah should get some presents too. The child's dad bent and whispered something to his son. A brilliant smile spread across the little boy's face, and he took his dad's hand and walked away, deep in conversation. A sudden wave of longing for her own dad, and her mum, washed over Janey.

An arm slipped around Janey's waist and squeezed. "Such wonderful news, isn't it, kiddo?" said Granny.

"Absolutely," said Janey, leaning into her grandmother. "I guess we're spending the night here," she added, looking at the snow pellets driving into the windows.

"We did the right thing," her grandmother said, giving her another squeeze. Together they watched as Santa heard the many wishes of the children. One little girl asked for her own goalie pads because her brother's were too smelly. Janey remembered how Michael's mum wouldn't turn on the car heater after a game so the smell of his pads wouldn't suffocate them all. She hoped he'd made it home before the storm started.

With the end of his elf's hat draped rakishly over one shoulder, Sam said something quietly to Charlie, who nodded. The elf announced to the room that it was time for Santa to leave. Night had crept up against the tall windows, highlighting the shifting, swirling patterns of snow brushing against the panes.

"Merry Christmas," Charlie called out, moving slowly toward the exit as little ones waved or rushed up for a final hug. When they reached the far end, Sam swept open a door and Charlie turned. "And to all a good night!" he declared, before disappearing from the hall.

Granny gave Janey another squeeze. "I'm going to go find my Santa," she said. "And it looks like someone's looking for you."

Glancing behind her, Janey saw Max – a beaming, elated Max – bounding toward her.

"He's fine. He's good," he said, sweeping Janey into a hug and spinning her around even as parents and tired, over-excited children tried to push past them.

"Let's get out of here," Max said, when he finally put her down. He pulled her by the hand along an empty hallway and turned to face her.

"Want to know what was really weird?" Janey nodded. "The detective who led the investigation? When my dad finally met her face to face, she was wearing a pin. With mountains on it. And the word *Banff* on the bottom. My dad said that his son was there right now, so she took the pin off, gave it to him and said that whoever wore it would have the strength of those mountains. Guess what was on the back?"

"Remember?"

Now it was Max's turn to nod. "And my dad says he'd never seen such a pin before." He looked at her searchingly. "We had to give Stefan the pin, didn't we? And tell him not to keep it. That was the key, right? It freed my dad."

"I'm not sure, Max. But I think we've done what we needed to do. No more time travelling for us. I'll bet we can push open any door in this hotel and we'll still be here, in

Banff, right now."

"This is a good place to be right now," Max said, moving closer. He hadn't let go of her hand. He gazed down at her. "Can I kiss you?"

Janey studied him. He was here, in front of her, tall and happy and grateful. But she sensed that part of him was already gone, back to his dad and his life in Vienna – a world she knew nothing about. She looked away. "I think..." She paused and gently pulled her hand from his.

"That we should dance?" Max filled in, as the opening notes of "Have Yourself a Merry Little Christmas" drifted down from the speakers.

She nodded. He took her hand again and drew her toward him. They swept effortlessly down the hallway, into a high-ceilinged room lit only by the cozy flames of its fireplace and the warm, white lights of a Christmas tree. When the song ended, Janey stepped back.

"You're such a great dancer," she said. "Thank you."

"And you're such a great friend," Max said. "Thank you."

They stared solemnly at each other for a moment. Not knowing what else to do, Janey curtseyed. Startled, Max bowed and then, unbidden, they both began to laugh. Loud and belly deep, their laughter grew and filled the room. They could not stop. If one of them managed to take it down to a few giggles, the other's convulsions set them off again. And just when they thought they'd wrestled themselves into control, Max's stomach growled, loudly. Off they went again.

They finally collapsed into two armchairs, wiping tears from their eyes. "I think we need to get something to eat," Max said finally. "I could eat a horse. Or a buffalo. Or anything right now."

Janey chuckled and nodded. "I also think we should track down the Olds. Who knows what they're up to."

"Does that worry you, if they get…close?" Max asked, suddenly sober.

Did it? She shook her head. "Nah. They ought to have a little fun too." She stood up. "Let's go find that buffalo. I hear they do a great bison burger here."

~~~

When Janey pulled back the curtains on Christmas morning, sunlight poured into the hotel bedroom. Snow was spread like thick, white icing across the landscape, and Janey wondered idly about the cookies she and Granny had decorated before they left for Banff. Maybe they'd have them tonight, once they got back home. She should wake her grandmother and start packing.

But the other bed was empty. Granny must have snuck out while she was still fast asleep. She checked the clock radio, surprised to see it was 10 a.m. She'd nearly slept through Christmas morning!

She yanked open the bedroom door. "Merry Christmas!" she called out. Several wrapped parcels peeked out from under the killer Christmas tree. The presents she'd bought for Granny, of course, were at home. But she knew Granny wouldn't mind.

Her grandmother was pouring herself a cup of coffee when Janey appeared. She set down the pot and held her arms open. "Merry Christmas, kiddo," she said, hugging Janey tight.

"Are Max and Charlie still asleep? Or is Charlie busy
~~~

shaving off his beard? And have you heard from Mum and Dad?" Janey checked the breakfast trolley, which was heaped with treats.

"No, no and yes," Granny said, going into the living room.

"Hmm. If the first no means they're not asleep, then where are they? I thought Charlie was finished with all his Santa duties." She picked up a piece of smoked salmon and stuck it in her mouth. Delicious. She could get used to living like this.

"He and Max are on an airplane," Granny said carefully. "Late last night Max found some flights to Vienna that left this morning. They're both flying over. Max will be with his dad by the end of the day. It'll be a wonderful Christmas present for them."

Janey looked up, a second piece of salmon forgotten in her fingers. "They're gone? They just left, without saying goodbye?"

"It was really early in the morning, Janey. Luckily, I was up to get a glass of water and I saw them off. Charlie and Max both apologized, but you can see how he'd want to go. And he left you something under the tree."

Janey wiped her fingers in a napkin and tried to unravel her feelings. After supper last night she and Max had barely had another moment alone. He'd spent much of the evening talking to relatives and making plans. The rescue of his dad, along with 14 victims of human trafficking, had made headlines. Friends who hadn't even known about the kidnapping were calling for details. When she'd gone to bed, he'd been deep in conversation with his Tante Grazia, reassuring her that all was well.

And all was well, Janey decided. Max was heading back to his dad, which is where he needed to be. If only –

"Don't you want to know more about my answer to your last question?" Granny had set out four plates and was bringing three more mugs to the table.

"Whoa, Granny, there's only two of us here. How much coffee are you drinking these days?"

"Go check the other bedroom."

"I thought you said –" But before Janey reached the bedroom door, it flew open.

"Surprise! Merry Christmas!" Janey's parents barely made it into the hallway before she reached them. They showered each other with fierce hugs and tearful kisses, filling the entry with joy and warmth.

"This is so, so great!" Janey blinked and wiped her eyes on her bathrobe. "When did you get here? How did you get here? Didn't the storm hold you back?"

"We flew into Calgary last night. The storm didn't reach there. And we caught a ski shuttle bus early this morning," her mum explained. "Granny told us that you couldn't get away from Banff, so we brought a little bit of Christmas here."

She hugged Janey again, then studied her daughter's face before releasing her. "I've missed you so much. And we have so much to catch up on." She tucked Janey's hand under her arm and guided her to the table. "But let's do it sitting down, over breakfast."

"Who wants some coffee?" Granny brought the carafe to the table.

They chattered and babbled and caught up on each other's lives. At one point, while Granny asked about her parents' travels, Janey put down her fork and beamed. They were all together. Not at home, but still, all together.

"I understand Santa was here," Janey's dad said finally. "But this is something from us. Well, Mum, me and Granny." He placed a gift beside her plate.

When Janey opened the box, she squealed. A new phone flashed at her. "This is the best!" She jumped up, hugging everyone around the table.

"I asked Nicky to upload your contacts and we had the store program it for you, so it's all set to go," her dad said, when she reached him. "It looks like you already have a bunch of texts waiting for you."

She checked her messages. Michael's name flashed across the screen. Just as she was about to open them, Granny put something else on the table.

"Max asked me to give this to you," she said.

Janey tore away the wrapping paper and discovered two clear bags. One was filled with caramel popcorn, the other with foil-wrapped chocolate balls. A card, with a photo of Cascade Mountain on it, peeked out from between the bags. Janey opened it.

> *I still owe you the pin, and I hope one day to give it to you in person. Thank you for everything. I will miss you. And I will remember.*
> *– Max*
>
> *P.S. When I talked to my Aunt Grazia last night, I remembered something. My aunt and great-aunt were both called Grazia. It's the German word for Grace. My great-grandfather always said the world can use more grace.*

Want to know more about Janey? Read about her earlier adventures in *Rescue at Fort Edmonton*, available where fine books are sold.

AUTHOR NOTES

Many of the events that Janey and Max encountered in Alberta's past are based on historical facts. The "discovery" of Banff's Cave and Basin by three railroad workers did lead to the creation of Canada's first national park, though Indigenous people in the area had, of course, long known about the hot springs.

Former citizens of the Austro-Hungarian empire were interned at Castle Mountain and later in Banff during the First World War. While most of these were Ukrainian, my own background compelled me to create two fictitious characters from Austria. During that same period, Banff celebrated Indian Days with parades and Indigenous competitions in the summers. To attract more tourists, the town also held its first winter carnival in 1917, complete with an ice castle built by those internees and a toboggan run along Caribou Street. The archives and library at the Whyte Museum of the Canadian Rockies are wonderful resources for those interested in the history of this area.

The consultations and conversations I had with Trent Fox, a member of the Stoney Nakoda Nation, offered me valuable perspectives and details to help me try to respectfully reflect the history of this First Nation.

Different written sources also provided me with information. They include:

The Stonies of Alberta: an illustrated heritage of genesis, myths, legends, folklore and wisdom of Yahey Wichastabi, the people who-cook-with-hot-stones, by Sebastian Chumak

"'Indians' Bygone Past': The Banff Indian Days, 1902-1945", *Past Imperfect*, 2, 7-28, by Laurie Meijer Drees

J.B. Harkin: Father of Canada's National Parks, by E. J. Hart

The Song and the Silence – Sitting Wind: The Life of Stoney Indian Chief Frank Kaquitts, by Peter Jonker

Banff: Canada's First National Park, by Eleanor G. Luxton

Spirits of the Rockies: Reasserting an Indigenous Presence in Banff National Park, by Courtney W. Mason

Blood and Salt, by Barbara Sapergia

These Mountains are our Sacred Places: The Story of the Stoney People, by Chief John Snow

The Rocky Mountain Nakoda website, at: rockymountainnakoda.com

"McDougall Orphanage and Morley IRS", from the United Church of Canada's Residential School Archive Project at thechildrenremembered.ca

Lastly, while the Banff Springs Hotel celebrates Christmas in grand fashion, not all the holiday events described in this book are real.

ACKNOWLEDGEMENTS

I am deeply indebted to Trent Fox, a member of the Stoney Nakoda Nation and researcher of the Stoney Nakoda language and history, for his thoughtful and careful reading of this manuscript. His invaluable consultation helped my efforts to portray the historical Stoney characters in this book in a respectful and accurate way. *Îsniyes*.

Though separated by many decades, Terisa Maxwell was the original Granny in the salon and kindly shared her story with me. Chris Standring gave me notes about how a mountain hotel Santa does his work. Kate Wiznura was always ready to answer questions about horses and horse-riding. Any errors in the book are mine.

Robert Feutl patiently walked me out of the dreaded time-travel loop. Thanks, brother mine.

Rob Alexander, Nicky Feutl, Warren Harbeck, Laura Mayne and Darian Selander read different sections and gave me great insights. My writer friends, including Caterina Edwards, Carolyn Fisher, Joan Marie Galat, Lorna Shultz Nicholson and Karen Spafford-Fitz, offered steady encouragement and awesome blue pencil advice. Thank you.

Finally, as always, my deepest gratitude to Sarah, Emma and Gordon. Without your patience, advice, re-readings and constant support, I would not be.

ABOUT THE AUTHOR

Photograph by Monique de St. Coix

Born in Toronto to parents who immigrated from Austria and Hungary, Rita learned English after she started school and discovered all the books in the library. She wrote her first story when she was seven.

Rita grew up to be a journalist, editor and teacher. She writes books for kids and young adults when she's not travelling or cycling or – best of all – travelling *and* cycling. *Rescue in the Rockies* was inspired by her discovery of a First World War internment camp memorial while cycling in Banff National Park.

Other books include *Rescue at Fort Edmonton* (the prequel to *Rescue in the Rockies*), *Room Enough for Daisy* and *Bike Thief*. Rita lives in Edmonton with her husband. You can learn more about Rita at www.ritafeutl.com.